S0-ADD-212

THE SECRET OF THE SWISS CHALET

Handsome Prince Rudolph Krisler's request for help in finding his family's long-lost heirlooms launch Jean and Louise Dana on a thrilling mystery while on vacation in Europe.

First, the young investigators' search is hampered by a mysterious young man who claims to be a member of the Krisler family. Next, a strange accident nearly costs Louise her life. Thoroughly mystified but equally determined to unmask their enemies, the girls follow a baffling trail of clues which finally leads them to an abandoned chalet in the Swiss Alps.

A trip to the St. Bernard Hospice, a perilous snowslide, a whirlwind escape on skis—all play an exciting part in solving this intriguing mystery.

Henri sprang forward and caught Jean.

The *Dana Girls* Mystery Stories

THE SECRET
OF THE
SWISS CHALET

By Carolyn Keene

GROSSET & DUNLAP
A National General Company
Publishers   *New York*

© 1958, 1973 BY GROSSET & DUNLAP, INC.
ALL RIGHTS RESERVED
PUBLISHED SIMULTANEOUSLY IN CANADA
LIBRARY OF CONGRESS CARD NUMBER: 72–90827
ISBN: 0–448–09087–2

PRINTED IN THE UNITED STATES OF AMERICA

CONTENTS

CHAPTER I

An Intriguing Case

"A PRINCE to see us!"

Seventeen-year-old Louise Dana, a pretty brunette, looked incredulously at the hotel manager who was standing in the doorway of the room which she shared with her sister.

"He does not call himself 'prince' any more," the manager explained quickly. "He is known as Rudolph Krisler. He would like to talk with you and your sister about a confidential matter and has requested permission to come up here."

Jean, Louise's blond-haired, vivacious sixteen-year-old sister, stepped forward. "In what country is Mr. Krisler a prince?" she asked.

"He's an Austrian by birth," the hotel manager replied.

Both girls were eager to meet the former prince and hear his story. They looked hopefully at their companion, Aunt Harriet Dana, for approval. She was chaperoning Jean and Louise and two of their Starhurst schoolmates on a vacation trip in Europe. Since the death of the girls' mother several years ago, Miss Dana had devoted her life to caring for the sisters.

Aunt Harriet, a petite, motherly looking woman, smiled. "We'd be very glad to talk to the prince," she told the manager.

After he had left, the girls and their aunt quickly tidied up the room. The coverlets of the two four-poster beds were smoothed and the personal belongings on the bureaus and desk hastily put out of sight.

"I hope the prince is charming," Jean said, giggling, as she surveyed the quarters which the Danas were occupying during their stay in the quaint hillside hotel on the outskirts of Frankfurt, Germany.

Louise smiled. "I think we should ask Evelyn and Doris to join us," she said.

When Jean nodded, Louise knocked on the door to the adjoining room. Doris Harland, an attractive blond girl, opened the door. Behind her stood Evelyn Starr, a dark-haired, slim girl.

"A prince!" Doris sighed when Louise made her announcement about the expected caller. "How romantic!"

"You would take that view of it," Evelyn teased. Being a serious-minded girl, she carefully considered every angle of any situation that arose. "Better watch your step, girls," Evelyn advised.

"I've heard there are a good many phony princes around."

The conversation was interrupted by a knock on the door. All the girls waited expectantly as Aunt Harriet called, "Come in!"

The door opened wide. Accompanying the hotel manager was a handsome, six-foot, blond-haired man about twenty-five years old. "Prince Rudolph Krisler!" the manager announced.

The prince made a low bow, then said that he was charmed to meet the Americans. "But, please, I am just Rudolph Krisler."

The manager introduced the Danas and their friends, then excused himself and closed the door.

As Aunt Harriet invited the prince to be seated in an old-fashioned, high-backed wooden chair, he said with a slight accent, "I hope you will pardon this intrusion. But I thought perhaps you could help me with a mystery."

Immediately the Dana girls' eyes lighted up. A prince and a mystery!

"I have traveled with your Uncle Ned several times and he has told me of the many cases you have solved. He suggested that I contact you."

Captain Ned Dana, of the transatlantic liner *Balaska*, lived with his sister and nieces.

As the young man paused, Louise said with a smile, "Please go on. Jean and I would rather solve mysteries than do almost anything else."

The prince said that he had a younger brother

named Henri. "When we were boys in Austria, trouble came to our country. It seemed best to my family to flee. Our heirlooms were quickly packed and sent ahead with two faithful servants. They managed to escape to Switzerland. We were to follow, but before we could leave, our parents died and we were too young to go alone."

"How sad!" Doris exclaimed sympathetically. "What did you and your brother do?"

Rudolph Krisler said they had been taken away by friends to a mountain retreat in Austria, and had remained there for several years.

"In the meantime, we tried to get some word from the servants," Rudolph continued. "Only two communications came through. The first told us where they were living and said that they had hidden the heirlooms. It is too bad they did not put them in a bank vault. The second letter was from some other refugees and brought the news that Anna and Fritz had lost their lives in a snowslide on the Jungfrau."

As the young man stopped speaking, his listeners expressed their sorrow at the tragedy.

In a moment Rudolph continued. "A couple of years ago my brother and I decided to visit the place where Anna and Fritz had lived, and try to unearth the family heirlooms."

"But you didn't find them?" Louise spoke up.

"Unfortunately, no. We located the chalet where they had lived. They called it Altberg, meaning Old Mountain. The heirlooms were not in it."

"There wasn't even one clue?" Jean asked.

For answer, the prince pulled a bulky envelope from his pocket. From it he extracted a small piece of paper and handed it to the Dana girls. In the center was a circle with uneven lines of varying lengths radiating from it.

"This may or may not be a clue. We found it with the first communication. It was among my father's papers. Henri and I could not figure out what it means. Can you?"

After studying the paper for several moments, Louise ventured the opinion that it might be a map. Rudolph agreed, but said he had no idea what it represented, since nothing to explain it had ever been found.

"Suppose I make a copy of it," Jean suggested, and went to the desk to do this.

As she handed back the original, Rudolph smiled broadly. "This means you will go to the Jungfrau and solve the Krisler mystery?"

Jean stopped short and turned around. She and Louise looked at their aunt questioningly.

"This all sounds most interesting," said Aunt Harriet, "but, Mr. Krisler, we must get the consent of my brother, who is the girls' guardian."

The prince nodded. "I'm afraid that I have let my enthusiasm run away with me, as you Americans say," he remarked. "I have no idea what your travel plans are, but I thought if you intended to go to Switzerland, you might include solving my mystery in your itinerary."

"We'd certainly love to," Louise assured him. "Aunt Harriet, suppose we cable Uncle Ned right away and ask him?"

Their aunt gazed thoughtfully out the window, then finally said, "Yes, we can do that." She turned to the prince. "We will let you know. Now please go on with your story."

Rudolph said that his brother Henri had become a Swiss citizen and was living in the chalet which Anna and Fritz had built. A Swiss couple were keeping house for him. "To support himself, Henri acts as a guide on the mountain. He will take you on climbs and ski trips over the glacier—"

"Oh, how exciting!" Evelyn broke in. Apparently her suspicion of the prince had vanished.

Rudolph stood up. "I must not take any more of your time," he said. "But I do hope you will be able to help my brother and me. If you decide to make the trip, I would suggest that you stay at Grindelwald. The chalet is up the mountainside from there." He smiled boyishly. "I will telegraph Henri that there is a possibility you may come."

Rudolph shook hands with everyone and left. Jean put the paper in her purse. Some time later Aunt Harriet suddenly remarked, "I wonder how your prince expects us to get in touch with him. He didn't give us any address."

The girls stared at one another and Jean remarked, "That's right. Well, he'll probably contact us later today or tomorrow."

"I think we should cable Uncle Ned immediately," said Louise, and offered to go downstairs to do this.

After sending the message, she stepped outside the quaint wooden building to take a short stroll. Some distance from the front doorway Louise noticed a bulky envelope lying in the roadway and hastened forward to pick it up.

Her eyes grew large with surprise. "Why, that's Prince Rudolph's envelope!"

On it was merely his name and a notation in German: "*Valuable papers.*"

"Oh, dear," Louise thought, "the prince will certainly be upset when he discovers his loss."

Hoping there might be an address inside, she opened the envelope. It contained many types of papers, mostly securities, and all bore the young man's name. But not one paper had an address on it. Louise went back to the lobby and asked the hotel manager where Prince Rudolph lived, but he did not know. She informed him of her finding.

"I'll just have to keep this envelope until we hear from him," she decided and went upstairs.

That evening when the Danas and their friends were ready for dinner, Doris went down first to mail some letters. As she reached the lobby the desk clerk called her over.

"Miss Harland, this is Herr Franz Dorfer," he said, indicating a large, beetle-browed man about forty-five years old. His hair grew low on his forehead, and his eyes were piercing. "Herr Dorfer has come for Mr. Krisler's envelope. He phoned and I said it was here."

"Oh!" said Doris. "I'll go upstairs and get it."

As she reached the second floor, Doris met Louise and Jean and told them of her errand.

"Who is this man who wants the envelope?" Louise asked.

"I don't know," Doris replied. "Does that matter?"

"It certainly does!" said Jean. "We wouldn't give up that envelope unless there was a letter from the prince with a certified signature!"

Doris looked hurt for a moment, but she realized at once how wise Jean's decision was. The three girls went down to the lobby and confronted Herr Dorfer. Louise asked the man for credentials, and the address and telephone number of Herr Krisler so that she might verify the request.

Herr Dorfer pulled himself up very straight and glared at the girl. "I am not in the habit of being questioned," he said in an ugly tone, and stormed out of the hotel.

Jean smiled. "That action makes him look like a phony," she commented.

"Yes," Louise agreed. "Unless Rudolph comes

in person for that envelope, I think we should turn it over to the police."

No further word was received that night from either Herr Dorfer or the prince. But early the next evening an answer came to Louise's cable. In it Captain Dana said:

> INVESTIGATION REVEALS MAN'S CLAIMS TRUE. LEAVE AT ONCE. FUNDS AT GRINDELWALD. MEET ME NEXT TRIP.

"We're going to Switzerland!" Louise cried out, dashing up to the rest of the group with the cable. "Uncle Ned is terrific!"

"He sure is!" said Doris. "Besides, he's the best ship's captain in the whole world!"

For many years, Uncle Ned had been captain of the *Balaska* which traveled the Atlantic between New York and Europe. It was he who had arranged the wonderful vacation abroad for his nieces.

The next few hours were busy ones. The hotel manager helped the Danas secure flight reservations for Switzerland and by the following morning the travelers were ready to leave.

Since they had a rented car for their stay in Frankfurt, it was agreed that Louise would drive the party and all their luggage to the airport. Then she and Jean would return the rented car and take Rudolph Krisler's lost papers to the police station.

After that, the sisters would get a taxi and join the others.

By nine o'clock Louise had discharged her passengers and the luggage, and then drove off to return the rented car.

"We'd better hurry!" Jean urged her.

Louise drove as fast as she dared and in a short while reached the rental garage. Then the two girls set off on foot for the *polizeiamt*.

As they hurried along and were about to cross the street, the girls were startled by the screech of automobile tires. As the car braked to an abrupt stop, two men jumped out and confronted the sisters. They recognized one of the men.

"Dorfer!" Louise and Jean exclaimed in unison.

Before either of the girls realized what was happening, Dorfer snatched Louise's purse and his companion grabbed Jean's. Then the men jumped back into their car and roared off.

CHAPTER II

A Plane Prisoner

THE GIRLS were stunned by the theft of their purses, but Jean recovered from the shock first and ran after the fleeing car, calling, "Stop, thief! Stop, thief!"

Louise, having seen something drop as Dorfer's companion jumped into the car, stooped to pick it up. It was a button, apparently torn from the man's coat when he had caught it on the door handle. She put the button in her suit pocket as she ran after Jean.

A woman driving a small sedan drove up alongside them and inquired if she could be of help.

"Oh, yes, thank you," Jean replied excitedly, and the two girls hopped in beside her.

"Please try to overtake that car," Louise pleaded. "The men in it stole our handbags! There are some important papers in them as well as our passports."

The Danas had been in tight spots many times

as the result of trying to help other people. In their recent mystery, *The Phantom Surfer*, the girls confronted many hazards in their attempts to trap the plotters responsible for the sabotaging of the restoration project at a seaside resort.

Now they were faced with the serious problem of being in a foreign country without passports and identification!

"Please hurry!" Jean urged their driver.

The woman driver wound in and out of traffic, blowing her horn continuously. Finally they spotted a policeman and quickly explained what had happened. The officer joined in the chase, and the distance between the two automobiles began to close.

Just as the car ahead rounded a corner, the Danas' handbags were thrown from the thieves' car. Instantly the girls' driver stopped, so that the bags might be retrieved.

Jean jumped to the pavement and ran to pick up the purses. Opening them, she made a quick examination, then said, "Everything is here except Rudolph's envelope."

She hopped into the car and the chase continued. But valuable time had been lost and the thieves' car soon was out of sight. The policeman suggested giving up the chase.

"Too bad!" said the obliging motorist. "Where may I take you?"

"To the *polizeiamt*, please," the officer requested.

In a short time the woman delivered her passengers to their destination. The policeman explained to the *wachtmeister* why they were there, then returned to his post.

After the girls told the police sergeant their story and described the two men, the *wachtmeister* said, "I think Franz Dorfer is an alias for a known international thief and smuggler, but I'll check with Interpol."

"That's the International Police Organization, isn't it?" Louise asked.

The sergeant nodded, then said, "Those papers in Prince Rudolph's envelope must be very important for the thieves to go to all that trouble. I'll try to find Mr. Krisler. If I do, I'll ask him why he thinks the papers were stolen."

"Have you any idea where the prince lives?" Jean asked.

The *wachtmeister* shook his head. Then he leaned forward and a twinkle came into his eyes. "Maybe you girls will solve some angle of this international smuggling ring. You seem to be involved in it already."

The Danas smiled politely, but the same worrisome thought was running through their minds. What was Rudolph's connection with it? Louise expressed her idea to the officer.

"Have no fear about the Krisler brothers," the *wachtmeister* said quickly. "They are very fine people and highly respected. This man who calls himself Franz Dorfer was trying to get hold of those papers for some nefarious purpose."

Louise glanced at her watch and said that if she and Jean did not hurry to the airport they would miss their plane. At once the *wachtmeister* offered to have a policeman drive them there. "Good-by and good luck!" he said, shaking hands with the girls.

The police car, honking and speeding through the streets, soon reached the airport. The girls went at once to find their aunt. She was standing with Evelyn and Doris, watching passengers board a plane bound for New York. The three were shocked to hear what had happened to the sisters.

"That dreadful man!" Doris cried out. "He might have spoiled our whole trip."

"Well, if he had kept our passports, it would have taken some time to get new ones."

The giant plane was almost ready for take-off. Suddenly a tardy passenger ran toward the gate, showed his ticket, and dashed through.

Louise stiffened. "Jean—that man— Wasn't he Dorfer's companion?" she exclaimed.

Without waiting for an answer, Louise dashed to the gate. The attendant asked for her ticket. Quickly Louise explained that she was not a passenger for the New York flight, but she must talk to the man who had just gone through the gate.

"Sorry, miss," the guard said. "No one without a ticket is allowed to go beyond here."

"But that man—he's wanted by the police! I can prove it!" Louise fairly shouted in her excitement.

The guard stared at her questioningly, then apparently realizing the seriousness of the situation, he said, "I'll send for a policeman."

Louise fumed as the seconds ticked off. Finally the officer arrived. The policeman looked grave as Louise finished her story. "This is a serious accusation, miss," he warned her.

"I know it is," Louise replied, "but I'm sure that man has some valuable papers that were stolen from my handbag."

"Come with me," the policeman said. "We will at least interview the man. That is, if you can make a positive identification."

He and Louise hurried through the gate and out to the plane. The officer spoke to the steward at the plane door. "Will you please ask that last passenger who went aboard to come here."

When the suspect emerged from the plane he glared at Louise and the officer and demanded to know why he was being questioned.

In a low tone to the policeman, Louise said, "This man is the one who stole my purse and valuable papers."

"I don't know what you're talking about," the stranger said. "I never saw this young lady before in my life."

Louise was staring at the man's jacket. One of the buttons was missing! Quickly she pulled the button from her pocket and handed it to the policeman. "If you need any further proof, here it is." Louise explained how she happened to have it.

The policeman took the man's arm, saying, "You must come to the office for questioning."

The man made violent objections. He asserted that he had important business to attend to in New York, and would have no more of this nonsense. As he started back toward his seat, the officer tightened his hold on the man's arm. "I would advise you to come without making a scene," he said.

"That man is wanted by the police!" Louise quickly explained to the attendant.

The prisoner had no alternative but to allow himself to be led from the plane, and his hand luggage went with him. Louise followed. As the group came back through the gate, Jean called out, "He's the thief all right!"

Louise quickly introduced her sister to the policeman, who asked both of them to accompany him to the office.

Concerned, Aunt Harriet spoke up. "How long will it take? Our plane leaves in ten minutes, officer."

"I'll ask that your plane be held up for another ten minutes," the policeman offered. "What is the number of your flight?"

On the way to the security office he stopped at the airline desk and made the request. The man in charge agreed to hold the plane.

While the stranger was being questioned and searched, the girls waited in the hallway outside the security office. Then they were called inside.

The policeman who had arrested him said, "This man is an American, traveling under the name of John Hudson. We have found nothing incriminating on his person or in his baggage. The papers you say were stolen are not here. Besides his clothes, his bag holds only a few purchases made in Europe—some perfume, leather goods, and these carved wooden figures." The officer held up one— an amusing-looking bottle stopper.

"You've got nothing on me and you can't hold

me," Mr. Hudson raged. "You've made me miss my plane. This airline will give me passage on the next flight, or I'll make trouble!"

"Not so fast, Hudson," the officer said. "I am turning you over to the city police for further investigation."

Jean glanced at her watch. The ten minutes were practically up! But before leaving she wanted to do a little detective work of her own.

Facing the prisoner and looking directly into his eyes, she asked, "Where is Prince Rudolph?"

"Why—he's—"

CHAPTER III

The Suspicious Guest

THE prisoner, John Hudson, realized that Jean Dana had trapped him into an admission. He stopped speaking and refused to go on. No amount of persuasion could induce him to talk.

The door suddenly burst open. Evelyn and Doris dashed in. "Your time is up, girls!" Evelyn cried out. "Hurry, or we'll miss the plane!"

The Danas quickly said good-by to the policeman, adding that they would keep in touch with the Frankfurt *polizeiamt*. A few minutes later they were on the sleek, giant airliner headed for Zurich.

"Well, this certainly was an exciting start to our trip," Doris remarked to Louise with whom she was seated. "I think it's simply wonderful the way you captured the criminal."

Louise grinned. "I've hardly got my breath yet."

After the stewardess had served lunch to all the passengers, she stopped to chat a moment with the girls while they ate the delicious German beef stew.

"Was the man you interrogated arrested?" she asked.

"Yes. He's a thief," Louise replied.

"I am glad you caught him," the stewardess said. When she came back later to talk with the girls she told them some interesting facts about Switzerland.

"You know four languages are spoken in the small country," she said. "In the southern part the people speak Italian, in the western section French, and in the Bernese Oberland where you're going they speak German. But everywhere the natives also speak English. They are taught it in school."

"Switzerland must be a fascinating place!" Doris exclaimed.

"I am sure you will find it so," the stewardess agreed.

When they landed in Zurich, the group discussed what means of transportation they would use to reach Grindelwald. It was decided they would hire a car with a driver who would explain the points of interest on the way. After making a few inquiries, they found a man who spoke excellent English and quoted them a fair price for the trip.

As they rode through the broad, tree-lined avenues of the busy city with its fine, stone buildings, Evelyn craned her neck out the window.

"Are you looking for somebody?" Jean teased.

Evelyn chuckled. "I've heard so much about men's Alpine costumes I want to see one. All the men I've seen are dressed just like American men."

The driver laughed. "You'll have to wait until we get into the country, miss. Then you'll probably see some mountain climbers."

Fifteen minutes later Evelyn had her wish. A handsome, sturdy young man in leather shorts and vest and wearing a white shirt and fedora with a tiny feather in it rode past them on a bicycle. He waved gaily and smiled.

When the travelers arrived in Lucerne, they were charmed by its beautiful lake and attractive shops.

Doris heaved a sigh. "I've lost my heart completely to Switzerland. And at the first opportunity I'm coming back to Lucerne and buy some things to take home."

They left the city and mile after mile of exquisite scenery went by. Presently the driver pointed out the snow-covered summit of the Jungfrau. "That's thirteen thousand feet in the air," he said. "You can climb up to it or take a train eleven thousand feet and hike the rest of the way. A railroad tunnel has been cut through three mountain peaks to get to the Jungfraujoch."

"It is perfectly beautiful," said Aunt Harriet. "And the air here—isn't it bracing and sweet?"

Jean, Doris, and Evelyn continued to exclaim

over the mountainous landscape. But Louise's face wore a serious expression. Finally she whispered to her sister:

"There's been a taxi back of us all the way from Lucerne. It may mean nothing at all. On the other hand, I don't see why the driver should speed up and slow down just as we do unless he is trailing us."

Aunt Harriet overheard the remark. "You're right, Louise," she said nervously. "I don't like this. I must insist that while we're on this trip we be especially cautious."

Presently the Danas' taxi pulled into the small, shining-clean town of Grindelwald. The girls were fascinated by the leaded-glass windows and dark-stained wooden buildings. When they reached the hotel Aunt Harriet registered for the group.

While she was busy at this task and a couple of bellhops were picking up the group's luggage, Louise kept eying the man who had alighted from the car that had been following them. It seemed to her that he was waiting deliberately for the group to leave before approaching the desk and registering. No one else was at the desk but still he did not step forward.

"Maybe I'm making a mountain out of a molehill," Louise told herself, "but I'm determined to find out why he's acting this way."

When her group left to go upstairs, she doubled back unbeknown to the stranger who now was talking to the desk clerk. She heard him say in German, "I have no reservation."

There followed a conversation which Louise did not understand. From the men's gestures, however, she assumed that the clerk was saying he had no accommodations and the stranger was insisting upon being given a room.

Finally the stranger said, "My name is Hermann Krisler."

Louise was startled. Was this man a relative of Rudolph and Henri Krisler? And was he trustworthy? If so, why had he acted so strangely? Louise hurried off and went up to the third floor where the Dana group had been assigned rooms.

"The plot thickens," Louise said, half smiling, when she joined the others in Aunt Harriet's room. "That man who was following our taxi is named Hermann Krisler."

"What!" exclaimed the others.

Aunt Harriet suggested that her niece might be unduly suspicious.

Suddenly Louise declared she was going to put on her hiking clothes and do some sleuthing.

"Are you going to follow this Hermann Krisler?" Doris asked.

"Oh, no," Louise answered. "That is, I won't follow him unless he acts suspiciously again. What I'd like to do right away is visit the Altberg Chalet where Henri lives."

Aunt Harriet put an affectionate hand on Louise's shoulder. "You and your sister have boundless energy," she said, smiling. "But you don't know this area yet and it's getting late. I suggest that you wait until morning before climbing the mountain."

"I guess you're right," Louise conceded, giving her aunt a hug.

The following day was a beautiful one with the sun shining brightly. The clouds which obscured an early-morning view of the top of the mountain soon dissipated. The girls put on sport shirts, sweaters, leather shorts, high socks, and stout shoes.

Aunt Harriet, who was not going to accompany them, looked at the group admiringly. "If you were only proficient in speaking German, I'd think you were natives!" she said, chuckling.

From the desk clerk Jean received directions to the chalet. She learned that it was possible to drive there on a winding road, but that by climbing straight up the mountain, the distance was shorter.

"Oh, we'll climb up," Jean said.

The girls started off, drinking deeply of the bracing air. After walking through the main street of the village, they set off up the mountainside.

Every fifty feet they would turn to admire the view. Wild flowers dotted the landscape—giant blue gentians, yellow auricula, white poppies, pink bird's-eye primrose. From the distance came the sound of tinkling cowbells. Here and there attractive chalets were set into the slope.

When the girls reached a height of five hundred feet, Louise remarked, "We must be almost there. That chalet to the right must be the Altberg."

The girls changed their direction and headed for the house. It was built entirely of wood and had highly ornate carving around all four sides beneath the unusually wide gables. On the roof small rocks had been fastened, evidently to keep the shingles from being blown away in a heavy wind.

The stone foundation was high and contained a heavy wooden door. There was a stone terrace which ran the full length of the chalet and above it a porch. Window boxes, filled with green vines and red geraniums, lent a cheerful, welcoming look to the dwelling.

"How perfectly charming it is!" said Doris.

Louise knocked on the door, which was opened by a smiling, middle-aged woman.

"Good morning," said Louise. "We are the Dana girls and these are our friends. Did you receive word from Prince Rudolph that we were coming?"

"Yes, I did," the woman answered. "Please come in. I am Frau Feer."

The girls followed her into an attractive, quaint living room. Sun streamed through the windows, bordered by ruffled, flowered curtains. Lovely hooked rugs lay on the floor, and the wooden furniture was decorated in multicolored designs of flowers.

"How is Prince Rudolph?" Frau Feer asked.

"We don't know, but we'd like to find out," Louise replied, and told her about the stolen papers. "May we have his address?"

Frau Feer answered worriedly, "I do not have it. Rudolph is a great traveler. He does not stay in one spot very long. Oh, I hope nothing has happened to him."

"We do too," said Louise, then asked, "Is Henri at home?"

The woman shook her head. "I am sorry," she said. "He took some tourists on a climb. But my husband is here and he would like to meet you, I know."

Herr Feer came in from the other room and shook hands with the girls. "I am delighted that you have paid us a visit and are going to solve the mystery of the missing Krisler heirlooms," he said, his bronzed, wrinkled face breaking into a friendly smile.

"We are looking forward to it," Jean told him. Then, noticing a glass-fronted cabinet in one corner of the room containing intricately carved wooden bottle stoppers, napkin rings, and other types of small articles, she asked whether the Feers collected them.

"*Nein, nein!*" Mr. Feer said, chuckling. "I make them to sell to the tourists."

The girls moved over to the cabinet for a better look at the wooden figures. Suddenly Louise noticed that one of them was exactly like the figure on the bottle stopper which had been in John Hudson's suitcase.

She asked, "Herr Feer, are these designs original with you?"

"Oh, yes," the man replied. "They are not sold anywhere else and I ask every customer who buys one to sign his name in my book."

The Dana girls exchanged knowing glances. Then Louise asked eagerly, "Was one of your customers named John Hudson?"

CHAPTER IV

The Missing Guide

HERR FEER shook his head. "That name is not familiar to me. But one minute. I get my book." He hurried out of the room and returned with a large leather-covered register. He ran his finger down the column of names. "No. No Hudson is here," he said.

When Louise explained that one of the men who had stolen Rudolph's papers from her had called himself John Hudson, the Feers were concerned. "What did this man look like?" the woman asked.

Louise described him as a heavy-set, square-jawed man of medium height.

"He had a tiny scar under his left ear," Jean added.

The Feers exchanged glances. "That could be a man who was here recently," said Herr Feer. "His name is Harold Rancher—at least, that is the way he signed himself. He is one of the tourists Henri has taken on a climb."

Herr Feer now opened the register again and showed the girls Rancher's signature. The thought occurred to Jean that it might be helpful to make a copy and send it to the *wachtmeister* at the Frankfurt *polizeiamt*. While the Feers showed the others the rest of the house, she took a piece of tissue from her purse and quickly traced the signature.

Meanwhile, Louise was asking the Feers when Henri would return. Frowns creased their faces. Then Frau Feer said, "Henri left here Sunday with two mountain climbers. We understood that he was to be gone only two nights, but we have not heard from him."

"Did he know we were coming?" Louise asked.

The woman nodded. "That is why we can't understand his not returning."

"Do you think he may have had an accident?"

"We are beginning to fear so."

Herr Feer said that Henri had been most eager to meet the girls and have them start solving the mystery. "The person who went with him besides Mr. Rancher was a young American named Fred Cox."

Louise, trying to be cheerful, remarked, "Perhaps the men Henri was guiding talked him into staying longer on the mountain. Since they came all the way from America, they probably wanted to do all the sight-seeing they could."

The girl's remarks seemed to ease the Feers'

tension. Frau Feer said, "You may be right. After all, Henri is not only an expert guide, but he is very strong and knows this mountain well."

Though the girls were worried that Hudson, alias Rancher, might have harmed Henri, they said nothing more about it, and turned to admire the room in which they were standing.

"Isn't this one of the most charming homes you have ever been in?" Doris asked enthusiastically. Noting the built-in bed with its high, rounded mattress and handmade blue-and-white quilt, she knew that underneath the quilt was a feather bed.

"This place is really beautiful," Louise agreed, as they reached the first floor again, and admired the heavy dark-beamed ceiling and the wide-board floor with its bright and quaintly designed hooked rugs.

The chairs intrigued the girls. They were made of wood and the backs had heart-shaped holes cut in them. They were painted black and each had a bright-colored bouquet of flowers near the top. On a large sideboard stood gaily decorated porcelain bowls and a pewter coffee service.

Frau Feer smiled at the girls' compliments. "I love the place, too. But I cannot take any credit for it. Anna and Fritz built the house and furnished it."

"Could you tell us something about them?" Jean requested.

The Feers said that they had not known the

couple. Rumor had it that they often went climbing high on the mountain. After a great snowslide, they had failed to return.

"These old mountains are beautiful," Frau Feer added, "but they can be dangerous, as well. One can never be too careful."

She invited the girls to join her and her husband at lunch. "Perhaps Henri will return before we have finished eating." The visitors accepted gratefully.

During the delicious meal of pressed meat, open Gruyere sandwiches and rich pudding, Louise asked if Henri Krisler had a relative named Hermann.

"I believe he does, but I have never met him," Mrs. Feer replied. "Do you know him?"

"No, not exactly," Louise said vaguely.

After helping with the dishes, the girls decided to return to the hotel. They asked Frau Feer to let them know when Henri returned.

"I will tell him to phone you," she said.

As the girls entered the hotel lobby, they heard a bellhop call out, "Mr. Frederick Cox. Telephone." A young man with dry, stringy blond hair and a very lean frame arose from one of the chairs.

Jean grabbed Louise's arm. "Frederick Cox!" she whispered. "Do you suppose he could be the same one who was up on the mountain with Henri?"

Louise, too, was startled. "Let's ask him and find out."

After the young man had finished his phone call, the Danas walked up to him. "Pardon me," Louise began, "but we heard your name called. Are you, by any chance, the Mr. Cox who was climbing the mountain with Henri Krisler?"

"Why, yes, I am," Mr. Cox replied.

"Did you just return?" Jean questioned him.

"Oh, no. I came down Monday morning."

By this time Doris and Evelyn had walked up. Frederick Cox stared searchingly at Doris. Uncomfortable, she looked away.

Louise introduced herself and the other girls, then said, "We've just come back from Henri's chalet. He hasn't returned yet. The Feers are very much concerned about him."

"Oh, I'm sure he's all right," Fred Cox said. "He's probably still with that other man."

"Who's that?" Louise asked.

"Mr. Rancher. I hardly know him."

"But," Doris burst out, "Mr. Rancher is in Frankfurt! In fact, he's—" The girl caught herself, realizing she should not have revealed this to a stranger.

Frederick Cox looked startled, and an expression of concern crossed his face. "I hope this doesn't mean Henri had an accident after leaving Rancher," he said.

Then, before the girls could comment on this,

Fred Cox suddenly took hold of Doris's arm and tried to lead her away from the group. When she pulled away, he leaned very close to her ear and said, "Lose your friends for a while, will you? I'd like to take you dancing."

"Thank you, but not now," Doris told him.

But Fred Cox was not to be dissuaded. "How about later tonight then?" he suggested.

"I'll be busy," Doris said firmly.

"Maybe you'll change your mind after you meet my mother and father," said Fred. "Here they come now. Dad's a swell guy and Mother's just out of this world."

As Mr. and Mrs. Cox approached, the girls saw that the man was an older edition of Fred. He had the same blond hair and washed-out looking blue eyes. Mrs. Cox was heavy-set, with dark hair and small, squinty brown eyes.

"Fred," she said in a scolding, petulant voice as she reached her son, "why won't you ever comb your hair?"

Fred paid no attention. Instead, he introduced Doris, then the other three girls. Mr. Cox, after bowing slightly, slapped Fred on the shoulder. "Son, I always said you were a good picker!"

The Danas and their friends were thoroughly disgusted. Mr. Cox was the type of American tourist they tried to avoid.

His wife proved to be just as crude. Giggling like a child, she said, "I simply adore Switzerland, don't you? But don't be fooled, girls. Don't let the robbers around here charge you fancy prices for things."

The girls made no comment. They moved toward the stairway to avoid any further conversation with the Coxes. Mr. Cox called out, "Fred is a lot of fun. Wait until you hear him sing and see him dance!"

Fred laughed. "Listen to this!" He struck a pose and began to yodel. The tune, instead of being a delightful Swiss air, was an American pop tune and the singer was off key. The result was so atrocious that the girls laughed.

Chuckling, Fred said, "You like it, eh?" and instantly burst into another tune, this one even worse than the preceding.

Evelyn could stand it no longer. "Help!" she said and dashed up the stairway.

Mrs. Cox burst out laughing. "Isn't that girl a comedian?" she said. "Well, Frederick, you go ahead and entertain these young ladies. Dad and I are going for a walk."

Fred Cox seemed determined to keep Doris and the Danas in the lobby. He stopped singing and his face became serious. "Don't mind the older generation," he said. "They sometimes go off the deep end about me. Say, you know, I've been thinking about Henri. Maybe I ought to go up on the mountain and look for him. How about you girls coming along?"

The Danas did not answer at once. The last thing in the world they wanted to do was climb the mountain with a pest like Fred Cox. On the other hand, something should be done about Henri.

"I believe," said Louise, "that the guide's disappearance should be reported to the police."

"Not necessarily," Fred spoke up instantly. "If Henri is all right, he'd be mighty embarrassed. The mountain guides here are very proud."

"Fred may be right, Louise," Jean said. "We don't want to do anything to embarrass Henri."

"All right," Louise agreed. "Maybe it would be better if we tried to find him first. Then, if we aren't successful, we can report the matter to the police."

"Atta girl!" Fred exclaimed. "Come outside with me and I'll show you the exact spot where I left Henri. You can see for yourself that it won't be a bad climb."

He led the way out of the hotel and a short distance along the side. Presently he stopped and pointed up to the gigantic slope.

"See that stand of cembra pine up there?" he said. When the girls nodded, he added, "It was right above there."

Louise started to speak, but broke off as a heavy object struck her on the back of the head. She swayed unsteadily for a moment, then fell to the ground, unconscious!

CHAPTER V

A Search Gets Under Way

"OH, LOUISE!" Jean cried out, and knelt beside her unconscious sister.

Doris looked down at the still form, terrified. "Is she—? Will she—?" Doris could not go on.

Fred Cox, meanwhile, was looking around to see who had thrown the object. "Hey, what's going on here?" he said. Then he stooped to pick up several pieces of the object which had broken when it hit Louise. "Hmm! This looks like some kid's piggy bank, only it's not a pig—it's a porcelain cow."

Jean glanced up at him, annoyed that he showed no concern over Louise. "Please help me carry my sister inside the hotel," she requested sharply.

By the time Louise was laid on the bed in her room, the girl's eyelids began to flicker and finally she opened them. "What—what happened?" she murmured.

"You were hit on the head," Doris replied. "Oh, I'm so glad you're all right."

When the hotel manager anxiously hurried in, Jean asked him to get a doctor. In a few minutes he returned with a young physician, who examined Louise's head and neck carefully. "I am sure she will be all right in a short time," he said. "But she must go to bed at once, and rest until morning." Turning to Louise, he smiled. "You are very fortunate, young lady. If the object which hit you had been made of metal, the blow might have been fatal."

Jean's mind was trying to find the answers to many questions. Had the object been thrown by some child who did not realize the consequences? Or had the porcelain cow been hurled deliberately by someone who wanted to harm Louise? Was it possible that Franz Dorfer was here?

After Louise had been tucked into bed, with Aunt Harriet acting as nurse, Jean said she was going to do a little investigating. She returned to the lobby and queried several guests who could speak English. None of them had seen the accident nor knew anything about a porcelain cow.

Finally the young sleuth went to the manager, who spoke several languages, and asked him to help her question various foreigners. He gladly consented. The first guests he approached were an Italian family. When he asked them about a porcelain *vacca*, they shook their heads vigorously.

"I will ask these French people," the manager told Jean. But when he asked them about *la vache fabriqué de la porcelaine*, they assured him they knew nothing about it. The German group was no more helpful. They had not seen the china piggy bank *kuh*.

"*Vacca, vache*, or *kuh*, I guess it's hopeless," said Jean. "But thank you just the same. You don't mind if I question some of your employees?"

"No, please do," the manager said. "They all speak English, so you'll have no trouble."

Jean decided to start with the chambermaids. She went from floor to floor on one end of the building without learning anything about the porcelain cow. In the section of the second floor directly above where the accident had occurred, she found a smiling, motherly chambermaid, who was carrying fresh linen to one of the bedrooms. The girl put her question.

"Porcelain cow," the woman said, looking off into space. She thought for several seconds, then her face lighted up. "This may help you a little. I empty all the wastebaskets from the rooms into a large container in that back hall. Yesterday I noticed an empty box in the container. A label on it said, *Porcelain Cow*."

Jean was excited. "Which room did it come from?" she asked eagerly.

"I do not know," the chambermaid replied. "In fact, someone may have dropped it directly into the big container."

Jean admitted this might be true, but she was inclined to think that the porcelain cow it had contained was probably owned by a person in one of the front bedrooms along the corridor. She asked who occupied them.

"Well," the chambermaid said, "several women and children traveling together have the end rooms. The two rooms between are occupied by people named Cox."

Cox! Was it possible, Jean wondered, that the Coxes had something to do with throwing the porcelain cow? She instantly put the thought from her mind because she knew Mr. and Mrs. Cox had gone walking just before the accident.

Jean thanked the chambermaid, then knocked on the door of the rooms occupied by the women and children. There was no answer. Disappointed, Jean returned to the first floor, determined to pursue her sleuthing along a different angle.

Using the house phone, she called Doris and Evelyn to come downstairs and help her. "I want to re-enact the accident," she said. "Let's go outside."

She asked Doris to stand in the exact spot where Louise had been when she was hit. "Now, let's see. The porcelain cow struck right here, from this angle." With her eyes, Jean drew an imaginary line upward to the second floor of the hotel. Her heart skipped a beat.

There was no question but that the porcelain cow had been thrown from a window in one of the Cox bedrooms!

"It certainly is mysterious," said Evelyn when Jean voiced her findings. "But you don't think the Coxes had anything to do with it, do you?"

Jean did not reply. Instead, she turned toward the hotel entrance, and the other girls followed her inside. Their attention was attracted to the desk. Mrs. Cox stood there, waving her arms around and exclaiming in a loud voice:

"Why, it's horrible—perfectly horrible! Suppose I had met the robber! Why, he might have murdered me for my jewelry! It's lucky for me I was out. But what am I going to do? My pearl necklace, two diamond rings, and a lot of other pieces are gone!"

"This is serious, very serious," the clerk said. "I will call the manager."

The manager came up and Mrs. Cox repeated her story. When she had finished, he expressed his sympathy and said he would call the police at once.

"In the meantime, I suggest that you make out a list of the jewelry which was taken," he said.

"I have it right here," said Mrs. Cox. "Oh, I just can't bear to go back into that room. It makes me shiver. You'll have to move me right away."

The manager said he was very sorry but that would be impossible. Every room in the hotel was taken.

Mrs. Cox burst into tears. Then, seemingly getting hold of herself, she said, "Well, I'll have to make the best of it. Never let it be said Hanna Cox is not a good sport!"

Doris took hold of Jean's arm. "Perhaps the thief who broke into Mrs. Cox's room threw the porcelain cow."

Jean nodded, as Evelyn suggested, "Maybe it was Dorfer or some friend of Dorfer's and Hudson's."

"There is even another suspect," Jean whispered. "Don't forget Hermann Krisler who seemed to have been following us here. I wonder where he is. I haven't seen him since our arrival."

Suddenly Jean snapped her fingers. "Oh! In all the excitement, I forgot to send that letter to the *wachtmeister* in Frankfurt and enclose the tracing I made of Rancher's signature."

She went to do this immediately. After mailing the facsimile of Rancher's signature, Jean hurried upstairs. She was anxious to learn how Louise was feeling and to report the results of her sleuthing. The color had already returned to Louise's cheeks and she laughed over Jean's account of trying to trace the porcelain cow in many languages.

"Maybe you should have tried Hindustani," she teased.

The following morning Louise declared that she had completely recovered from the accident and insisted upon going back to the chalet to find out whether or not Henri had returned.

"Well, if he hasn't, the Feers should report it to the police," Jean said firmly.

"How about Fred Cox?" Evelyn asked, eying Doris.

"Let's forget him," Jean replied. "At least until we talk it over with the Feers."

The girls wore sweaters, warm ski pants, and carried jackets with them. They tucked some Swiss chocolate bars in their pockets as emergency rations.

"Promise me you'll be very careful," Aunt Harriet pleaded as the girls prepared to leave their rooms.

"We will," Louise and Jean promised, giving their aunt a tight hug.

When they reached the lobby, Jean stopped at the manager's office to inquire whether there was any clue to the person who had hit Louise, and if there were any trace of the thief who had taken Mrs. Cox's jewelry.

"None at all," the man replied. "But the police are looking into both matters."

As the other girls waited for Jean, they saw Fred Cox coming toward them. He was dressed in mountain-climbing clothes.

"Good morning, good morning," he said cheerily. "It looks as if you and I were going in the same direction. That's the way it should be. I thought you'd come around to my way of thinking and let me show you the spot where Henri might be trapped."

The girls were silent. They glanced at one another and it was not until the pause became embarrassing that Louise spoke up.

"Perhaps you're right. We'll stop first at the Altberg Chalet. If there's no word from Henri, then we'll go with you up the mountain."

"Now you're talking sense," Fred said. Taking Doris's arm, he added, "You come with me."

Doris looked annoyed, but to avoid any unpleasantness took his outstretched hand to be led from the hotel. The others followed quickly.

At the chalet they learned from the Feers that there still had been no word from Henri. The Swiss couple was relieved to learn that the girls were going to make a search for him, and that if they did not find him quickly, the matter was to be reported to the police.

"Henri's cousin Hermann was here," said Frau Feer. "He had heard about Henri not returning. He was very worried too about him, and has gone up the mountain on a hunt."

"Hermann Krisler tried to get a room at our hotel," Louise observed.

"They could give him a room for only one

night," Herr Feer said, smiling. "He has moved in here."

The Danas hoped that it did not mean trouble for Henri. The sisters had a very uneasy feeling about the whole situation.

Louise, on a pretext of wanting a drink, asked Frau Feer if she might go into the kitchen for a glass of water. In the kitchen Louise whispered that she had an unusual request to make.

"As you know, we girls are not familiar with the mountain," she said. "Fred Cox pretends to be, but I don't trust him. If you don't mind, would you let me fill my pockets with rice? I'll drop a few grains as we go along, so we can find our way back." Frau Feer gladly gave her a boxful.

Jean, sensing that something important was afoot, came into the kitchen. She and her sister filled all their pockets, then returned to the living room.

Herr Feer insisted upon giving the young mountaineers a coil of rope and some climbing sticks. "You may need them, and it's always safer to have them along. If it were not for the stiffness in my right knee caused by a fall last month I would go with you."

Fred led the girls on a zigzag course up the mountainside. Despite the gravity of their errand, they found themselves pausing every little while to admire the beautiful scenery.

During one of the stops, Doris flung her arms wide and cried, "Oh, doesn't this air make you feel absolutely wonderful? And just look at that view!"

The lush grass was dotted with blue gentians and white anemones. Below them in the distance were lakes and towns, and above them green fields leading to the crags and snow fields. Far to their right was the railroad which wound up the mountain and finally disappeared into a tunnel on its way to the Jungfraujoch.

As soon as Louise was out of sight of the chalet, she began leaving a trail of rice. "I must use it sparingly," she thought, "and not run out of it."

Presently the climb became more difficult. The grass was sparser and there were outjuttings of rock. Now and then they came to a ravine which they found it necessary to skirt.

"How are you doing?" Fred called back once. From time to time he had assisted Doris, but paid hardly any attention to the other girls.

"Everything's fine," Louise replied, then said, "Listen!" From a distance had come a cry, "*Hilfe!*" Though it was in German, there was no mistaking the fact that someone was in difficulty and needed help!

CHAPTER VI

A Mountain Rescue

THE GIRLS and their companion halted and listened intently for the cry for help to be repeated. In the vastness around them, none was sure from which direction the plea had come.

But though they stood perfectly still and strained their ears, there was not a sound on the mountainside. Finally Fred Cox began to call "Hello!" in a loud voice. There was no answer.

Doris looked worried. "I hope we're not too late. Do you suppose the person who called for help could be Henri?"

At once Louise remarked that whoever it was, they must do their best to find the person and rescue him. At Evelyn's suggestion they spread out in various directions.

"We mustn't get far apart, though," Louise cautioned, and the limit was set at two hundred feet from the starting point.

The hunt went on for some time, with each

of the searchers calling at half-minute intervals. Each came almost to the two-hundred-foot limit and still there was no answering call from the victim.

"Hello! Hello!" Evelyn shouted once more at the top of her voice.

Suddenly, to her relief, she heard a muffled answer. The person was not far away! In a few moments Evelyn came to a deep rocky ravine. She hurried up to the rim of it and looked down.

At the bottom, wedged between two rocks, was Hermann Krisler!

"Get me out of here!" he demanded.

"All right," Evelyn replied. "I'll bring my friends. We have a rope with us. I'm glad we found you."

"Well, it's about time somebody came," Hermann Krisler remarked tartly.

The girl frowned. This seemed like pretty ungrateful talk from one in such a helpless position!

Evelyn went part way back toward the spot where the group of searchers had separated, calling their names as she went. One by one, the others answered and came toward her. Quickly they followed Evelyn to the rocky ravine and looked over the edge.

"Hurry up! I can't stay here all day!" Hermann Krisler called out. "I have been cramped up too long as it is."

"Well, how do you like that?" Fred Cox said.

He called down, "What ails you, beefing like that with four beautiful girls coming to your rescue?"

The Danas were already uncoiling the rope that Fred Cox had been carrying. One noose was slipped around a pinnacle of rock some distance back from the rim. The other end was sent down to Hermann Krisler.

"Can you get the noose under your arms?" Louise called to him.

Wedged as tightly as he was, it was hard for the man to do this. He grumbled and complained continuously, but finally he raised his arms above his head and managed to get the noose under his shoulders. The rescuers got in line, grasping the rope. Evelyn was in front.

"Ready?" she asked him.

"Yes. But take it easy. I don't want you to break my arms."

Doris, completely disgusted, whispered to her friends, "It would serve him right if we left him down there!"

Slowly, the group at the top of the ravine began to haul up the rope. For a few moments it looked as if Hermann Krisler's feet were too tightly wedged for him to be released, but after he had twisted and turned his body many times, his feet finally came free from the rocky crevice. Those above him sighed in relief and pulled on the rope faster.

Evelyn, in her eagerness, leaned down too far

and suddenly lost her balance. The edge of the rim crumbled, and in trying to save herself from falling, she let go of the rope. Down, down she slid to the bottom of the ravine!

"Oh!" Doris screamed.

Fortunately, Evelyn missed the deep crevice which had imprisoned Hermann Krisler. She picked herself up and to the others' amazement laughed! "Want to try a toboggan anybody?" she asked.

"No, thanks," Jean replied.

As soon as Hermann Krisler was brought to the rim, he removed the noose from under his arms and it was thrown down to Evelyn. She adjusted it quickly and was brought to the surface.

"Thanks a million," she said gratefully, embracing the other girls.

"How about me?" Fred Cox smirked.

Evelyn shook hands with him. Then introductions were exchanged with Hermann Krisler.

"I understand that you are here trying to find your cousin Henri," Louise said.

"Yes, I am very worried about him," the Austrian replied.

"We're looking for him too," Louise went on. "Fred has an idea where he may be. Do you want to join us or go back?"

"I will go along," Hermann answered.

After a short rest, the group plunged on. The climb was becoming more and more difficult and

breath-catching stops were made every ten minutes.

"I feel as though I were getting nearer the top
of the world all the time," Doris remarked. "And
these flowers! They grow without any soil at all,
it seems!"

The panorama was widening and becoming more
gorgeous. Fred pointed to tiny white flowers cling-
ing to inaccessible crags. "That is the famous
edelweiss—national flower of Switzerland. They
tell me some people actually risk death to pick it.
Crazy, I say!"

Louise had fallen behind with Hermann. Presently he asked, "Do you know my cousin Henri?"

"No, but I've met his brother Rudolph."

"Where was that?"

"In Frankfurt," Louise replied. She glanced sideways at her companion, wondering how much she
should tell him. Deciding to be wary, she asked,
"Are you and Henri and Rudolph first cousins?"

"Oh, yes," Hermann answered. Then he urged
Louise to tell him more about Rudolph whom he
had not seen for some time.

In reply, Louise inquired if Hermann knew two
men named Dorfer and Hudson. When he said no,
she told him about the stolen envelope.

Hermann muttered something in German under
his breath, then said to Louise in English, "I hope
those papers did not concern the Krisler estate.

Slowly they began to haul up the rope.

There are a large number of heirlooms which we are trying to find."

The man explained that the heirlooms had belonged to the cousins' grandparents, who had willed them to the three boys. Louise did not comment on this, but the story certainly was not the same as the one she had heard from Rudolph.

"In fact," Hermann concluded, "I was to receive half of the heirlooms. Rudolph and Henri were to divide the rest."

Louise was astounded to hear this. Was Hermann's story true? She had no way of knowing, but intuition told her that it was not.

She began to grow uneasy about the whole affair and to review the case. The man who called himself Rancher, and was probably Hudson, was in Frankfurt on Tuesday. There was just a chance that an accident had befallen Henri after Rancher had left him on Monday. It was possible that Hermann Krisler had had something to do with it!

"Oh, I mustn't think about such things," Louise scolded herself, and tried to shake off the mood.

Her attention was distracted by the sounds of yodeling ahead. For an instant she thought Fred Cox might be singing one of his solos. But within a few seconds she realized a native Swiss was coming down the mountain in their direction. The sweet, clear warbling was beautiful.

As the yodeler approached, Doris gasped in delight. The man wore the regulation leather shorts, embroidered jacket, and tiny feathered hat which she had seen in photographs of Switzerland. His eyes were sky blue, his skin deeply sun-tanned, and his cheeks were ruddy. "Oh, isn't he handsome!" Doris said under her breath.

"Wait'll you see me in a suit like that," Fred Cox spoke up.

"*Guten Morgen*," the yodeler said as he came up and stopped.

Hermann Krisler spoke briefly to the Swiss in German, then turned to the others and said the man had not seen Henri on the mountainside.

"Oh, you are Americans," the yodeler said in English. "I am sorry if your friend is in trouble and I hope you find him. If not, I suggest that you report the incident immediately."

"We will do that," Hermann Krisler told him.

The yodeler started off. Almost at once Fred Cox began to try imitating the mountaineer. Doris covered her ears and begged him to stop.

Fred merely laughed and went on. Jean, her eyes twinkling, decided that the only thing to do was to drown out his singing by yodeling louder. Taking the lead, she encouraged the other girls to follow. To everyone's astonishment, Evelyn proved to be an excellent yodeler.

"You sound like a native," said Hermann.

The competition was too much for Fred. As

soon as he became silent, the girls too stopped yodeling.

Once more Hermann Krisler fell behind with Louise. "Who is this man Cox?" he asked.

"I really don't know," Louise answered, "but he is the type of tourist that the United States is not proud of."

"I can see why," Hermann remarked. "Can't we get rid of him? Send him back to the hotel, and then we can talk freely about the Krisler heirlooms without him hearing us."

For a second Louise was tempted to do this, thinking she might pick up some valuable clue from Hermann, but almost instantly she decided against the move. She did not know this man any better than she knew Fred Cox and deep in her heart she mistrusted both of them.

Since leaving the last chalet behind, Louise had been dropping grains of rice along the way. Neither man was aware of this, and it gave Louise a slight sense of security. Presently she left Hermann and went forward to climb with Jean. She whispered that her pockets were empty and requested her sister to start dropping some grains of rice.

"I'll go up ahead and ask Fred what spot he's heading for," Louise said. "We passed that landmark of the clump of pines a long time ago."

Upon reaching their leader, she put her question to him. Fred did not reply for several seconds. By this time they had rounded an outcropping of rock. He pointed some distance ahead.

"See that little hut?" he asked. "That's where I left Henri Krisler with Mr. Rancher."

Fred explained that the three men had climbed much higher and gone down to spend Sunday night at the hut. "The next morning I was ready to quit. But Rancher wanted to go on, so I left him and Henri at the hut."

The group scrambled up over the uneven terrain until they reached the cabin. Fred called loudly, "Anybody home?" There was no answer, so he pounded loudly on the door. No one came to open it.

"Is the door unlocked?" Louise asked, her heart pounding.

It yielded to Fred's turn of the knob and he swung the door wide. The searchers were almost fearful to look inside, wondering what they might find.

CHAPTER VII

A Mysterious Struggle

As THE group stared into the interior of the mountain cabin, they could see little.

"It's spooky," Doris murmured. "Let's wait and have Fred take a look."

But the Danas stepped inside with Fred. As their eyes became accustomed to the dim light, they could distinguish several bunks, a table, and two chairs. In one corner was a crude stove with pine logs piled up beside it.

"No one here," said Fred Cox. "Well, I guess this is the end of the trail. We may as well go back. I have a date, anyway." He looked at Doris, who stood in the doorway. "But I'll break it if you'll go out with me tonight."

"I'll be busy myself," Doris replied.

During the conversation, Louise and Jean had been looking around the hut. Suddenly Jean pounced on a note which lay face up on one of the bunks.

"It's in French!" Jean exclaimed. "But I think I can read it." Slowly she translated:

" *'If anyone finds this note after tomorrow, the tenth, it will mean I have not returned home because I have had an accident, perhaps not through my own fault. My companion and I, Mr. Rancher, are taking a straight route northwest of here. We shall climb for two hours, then descend.'*

"It's signed 'Henri Krisler.' "

The sisters looked up from the paper and stared at each other. So Henri had suspected possible foul play, they both thought!

By this time the other girls and Hermann had entered the hut. The note was read to them. Instantly Doris and Evelyn expressed their fear that Henri might have had a fatal accident.

"Or one that wasn't fatal," Jean said quickly. "In any case, we mustn't stop searching."

"Of course," said Doris.

"Not me," Fred Cox announced determinedly. "And I'm not going to let you girls risk your lives, either. The climb from here is very dangerous. Take a look yourselves."

The girls walked outside and gazed in a northwesterly direction up the mountain. There was no question but that Fred Cox was right. For a short distance the going would not be too bad, but soon it became sheer rock.

"I feel very bad about Henri," Hermann spoke up, "but I guess this time he took one chance too many. There is no point in the rest of us risking our lives. When we get back to the village, we'll notify the authorities."

The Danas looked intently at Hermann Krisler, wondering how he could be so heartless!

Fred Cox showed no concern. "I've done my bit," he said. "Let the police send a helicopter to take a look."

Without further ado the two men began the downward trip. Doris and Evelyn started to follow them, but the Danas hung back.

"Wait a minute," said Louise.

"You'd better come," Doris advised. "We don't want to be left up here alone."

Evelyn was torn between a desire to stay and a feeling that it might be disastrous not to leave with the men. Finally she decided to follow Doris. "Louise! Jean! Come on!"

The sisters held a whispered conversation. Both had come to the conclusion that if Rancher, or even Hermann had intended to harm Henri Krisler, he would not have waited very long after leaving the cabin.

"There's a slim chance Henri isn't far away," Louise declared.

"Yes," said Jean. "I think we should climb as far as we dare and keep looking."

Louise agreed. "I'd never forgive myself if I didn't try," she said determinedly.

When Evelyn and Doris realized that the Danas

were not following them, they returned to the hut. The situation was explained to them, and at once both assented to go along. Jean picked up the coil of rope which Fred had dropped on one of the bunks, and swung it over her left shoulder.

The girls went outside and gazed after the retreating men. By this time they were a good distance down the rocky slope, and apparently were disinterested in whether or not the girls joined them.

"Those men don't have the manners of an earthworm," Evelyn burst out in disgust.

"What's even worse, I think," said Jean bitterly, "is that they're such poor sports. They should have kept on searching as far as the danger line before giving up."

"I agree," said Louise. "Come on!"

The four girls dug their hiking boots into the pebbly, rocky ground. Progress was slow, but they kept on doggedly.

Finally Louise, in the lead, stopped. "I believe we've gone as far as we dare without more climbing equipment and an expert guide."

"Let's try shouting Henri's name," Jean proposed.

The girls took turns, the sound of their voices reverberating from the mountain. There was no reply.

"I hate to admit defeat," said Doris, "but I guess we'll have to give up."

"Oh, girls, look!" Louise cried out suddenly.

At the same moment she stepped a few feet to the right, leaned down, and picked up a small object.

"What is it?" the others asked eagerly.

Louise displayed one of the Feers' ornamental wooden bottle stoppers. There was no question in anyone's mind now but that the climbers had come this far at least.

"You think Henri dropped it as a clue?" Evelyn asked, taking fresh hope.

"It could have been dropped by either Henri or Rancher," Louise mused. "Remember Herr Feer said Rancher had purchased some. The two men may have had a tussle here and the bottle stopper dropped from the pocket of one of them."

A struggle! The girls pondered this. If it had taken place here and Henri had been the loser, he should be somewhere in the vicinity!

The girls spread out and began an intensive search. Over and around the rocks they climbed, looking in every nook and cranny. Five minutes went by, ten, fifteen—

"I've found him! I've found him!" Jean suddenly cried out excitedly. She was standing on tiptoe looking into a pit below, her left arm hugging a slender, jagged rock for support.

The other girls rushed to Jean's side. Sprawled on the rocky ground below was the figure of a man in mountaineer's garb. He looked so much like Rudolph Krisler that the girls were positive this was his brother Henri.

"Oh, how dreadful!" Doris exclaimed. "Do you —do you think he's still alive?"

No one answered, but they looked at the still figure intently.

His hands were bound and a gag had been tied across his mouth. As they watched, the girls could detect a slight raising and lowering of the young man's chest.

"He's breathing! He's alive!" Jean shouted.

"We must hurry and rescue him," Louise urged.

"It's not going to be easy to get to where he is," Doris spoke up, as the four girls surveyed the almost sheer drop of some twelve feet.

"Suppose you let me down on the rope," Jean suggested.

She swung it off her shoulder and adjusted one of the loops under her arms. She was slowly lowered.

Evelyn remarked, "Herr Feer's rope has really been a lifesaver. Whoever would have thought we'd use it twice in one day?"

When Jean reached the floor of the pit, she instantly removed Henri's gag and bonds. The guide stirred slightly but did not regain consciousness.

"I don't think any bones are broken," Jean called up after a cursory examination. "I think he's suffering from hunger, thirst, and exposure."

"How are we going to get him up?" Doris asked, perplexed.

Jean suggested that they improvise a stretcher to support him. "Then we'll tie the ends of the rope to it." She unfastened the noose from her shoulders and Louise lowered the one on the other end of the rope, holding tightly to the center of it.

Meanwhile, the three girls at the top of the pit securely tied their ski jackets together by the sleeves and belts. They tossed the crude stretcher down to Jean, who added her own jacket to the others.

First, she placed the makeshift litter under the victim, then slipped one noose of the rope under Henri's knees. Next, she tied the other end to the two sleeves of the jacket which held his head.

"Ready! Hoist!" she ordered. "But do be careful!"

The three girls at the top began the slow haul. They thought the joggling and scraping against the side of the pit might awaken Henri, but he remained motionless. Finally, he was brought to the rim in safety. The rope was sent down once more and soon Jean was standing beside the others.

"Let's try a little massage," Louise suggested.

But though they rubbed Henri's wrists and the back of his neck, there was no sign of returning consciousness.

"We must get him back to the chalet as quickly as possible," Louise said.

Suddenly Doris wailed, "Back to the chalet! How in the world are we ever going to find our way without Fred Cox?"

"Oh, Louise took care of that," Jean spoke up. From her pocket she took a few grains of rice and told the other two girls of Louise's precaution.

"Thank goodness!" Doris said.

The four girls each took a corner of the stretcher, with Jean and Evelyn in front, and started following the path of the rice. The descent was slow and arduous. Once Henri groaned loudly and the four girls watched him intently. They were sure he was going to regain consciousness. But a moment later he became quiet again and remained in the deep sleep.

"Maybe we were hurting him," Evelyn suggested.

From then on, the girls were extremely careful not to jar him as they went on and on.

After the rescue group had walked for nearly half an hour, they came to a point where the trail of rice disappeared completely. Doris looked worried, but Louise explained that she remembered turning a sharp corner at this point.

As they took a left-hand turn, the girls were confronted by a large, menacing-looking goat. The startled girls stopped. The next moment, the buck lowered his horns and bounded toward them and their burden.

CHAPTER VIII

The Secret Shelf

THE GOAT was only a few feet away when Jean cried out to Evelyn, "Quick! Take my side of the stretcher too!"

Evelyn moved quickly and grabbed the other jacket sleeve. Jean ran forward, waving her arms and yelling at the top of her voice. Seeing this strategy to hold off the animal, Louise instantly handed her part of the stretcher to Doris and also dashed toward the goat. Together the sisters managed to frighten him into changing his course. He lurched sideways and came to an abrupt stop.

"Hurry! Run!" Jean called to Doris and Evelyn.

The two girls sped off, the stretcher swinging violently between them. Meanwhile the Danas, trying to imitate the tactics of a matador, kept luring the goat on, then side-stepping as he was about to butt. Their idea was to keep him in this spot until Doris and Evelyn were at a safe distance with their burden. Nimbly they backed and dodged, always keeping the goat going in a circle.

Finally a smile came over Jean's face. "Louise, I think this old fellow is just being playful. He doesn't intend to hurt us at all!"

"Just the same, I don't want to get too near those horns!" Louise replied. "Let's make a run for it."

The sisters deliberately kept the animal headed in a direction away from the one which Doris and Evelyn had taken. Then suddenly they turned and hurried down the mountainside. The animal did not follow.

As Louise and Jean caught up to the other girls, they resumed their positions at the stretcher. "Whew! That was a close one!" said Doris. "I'll be glad when we reach the chalet."

The descent down the mountain was an arduous one. Henri began to groan as though in great pain. The girls paused to discuss what to do. Should they stop often so as to disturb the patient as little as possible? Or should they hurry and get him to a doctor?

"I suggest we go quickly to the nearest chalet and phone from there," Louise said.

At last they reached a dwelling and knocked on the door. There was no answer.

"We may as well go all the way," Louise decided. Determinedly the stretcher-bearers pushed on. When they reached the Altberg Chalet, Frau

Feer, who was picking flowers in the garden, rushed toward them. "You have found him! *Ach, ja!* I am so happy!" She called loudly for her husband.

With the Feers taking charge, Henri was put to bed in his first-floor room. In a few minutes Frau Feer came out.

"Papa has done a little doctoring," she said to the girls. "He says that no bones are broken and there are no head injuries. Henri is lucky."

She went on to say that her husband thought Henri was regaining consciousness and should have some nourishing broth, then Frau Feer went to the kitchen. After she had carried the steaming hot broth into the sickroom, Frau Feer came to sit down with the girls. But a moment later she jumped up.

"Oh, how forgetful of me!" she said. "You must have some of the broth, too, and a good dinner."

Soon the weary girls were sipping the delicious beef soup and eating large slices of Frau Feer's homemade bread on which had been spread creamy butter and wild-strawberry jam. This was followed by fricassee of chicken with dumplings.

"This is delicious, Frau Feer," said Louise. "By the way, where is Hermann Krisler?"

"He went down to the village for a haircut."

"Good."

As the girls finished the main part of the meal,

Herr Feer came from Henri's room. There was a smile on the man's face as he said, "Henri is conscious now. He insists upon meeting you girls. He wants to thank you for rescuing him."

Louise turned to Frau Feer. "Do you think we should go in? Isn't it rather soon?"

The woman smiled. "If Papa thinks it is all right, then it is all right," she told the girls.

Despite this, Doris and Evelyn spoke up and insisted that the Danas go first. They would meet Henri later.

Herr Feer led the way. To the sisters' astonishment, Henri Krisler was sitting up in bed, with several oversized feather pillows behind his back. Louise and Jean were amazed at how well he looked. The thought rushed through their minds that a person with a fine physique and in good health could make a very quick comeback after a harrowing experience.

When Louise and Jean walked forward, Henri Krisler put out both his hands and shook theirs fervently. "This is a most undignified way to make your acquaintance," he said, chuckling. His voice was deep and musical. "I assure you my plans were quite different. I never intended that you should find me unconscious on the mountain!"

The sisters smiled. "We were so relieved to find you alive," said Louise, "that we forgot everything else." To ease the situation, she told him the story of the goat.

Henri laughed merrily. "So I must thank you for saving my life twice," he said. "I don't know which would have been worse—to be butted to death or left to die in a pit."

Frau Feer came in with more food for the patient and the Danas offered to leave. But Henri would not hear of this. He insisted upon meeting Doris and Evelyn, then told the girls his story.

He said that after Fred Cox had left the hut, Rancher had begun to talk about the missing Krisler heirlooms. He insisted that he had received information from someone as to where they were buried. If Henri would promise him a share of the find, Rancher would reveal the information.

"Do you think he was telling the truth?" Evelyn asked.

Henri shook his head. "I felt sure that he was lying. But I played along and said that of course anyone who located the heirlooms would be well paid. So he said to follow him. I was suspicious of his intentions and that is why I wrote the note."

Evelyn asked, "Was there any significance to your writing it in French?"

Henri explained that he had done this because more people read and understood that language than any other. "How fortunate for me you could read it. I am not surprised that you ask, though, since I was born in Austria. Did Rudolph tell you that I am now a citizen of Switzerland? Otherwise, I could not be a mountain guide. However," he went on, "that was not my reason for becoming a citizen. Switzerland is a wonderful place in which to live and there are no finer people in all the world than the Swiss." Henri looked affectionately at the Feers, who smiled and bobbed their heads.

"Please tell us what happened after you left the note," Jean begged.

"Mr. Rancher told me," Henri went on, "that according to a report he had, the heirlooms were buried in a certain section higher on the mountain. It was in a northwesterly direction from the hut."

Doris spoke out in disgust. "That awful man deliberately lured you to the pit and attacked you!"

"That's right," Henri admitted ruefully. "Rancher is very strong—he has muscles like iron. This, together with my being taken by surprise, put me in a bad position. He was walking ahead of me when he suddenly turned and gave me a knock-out blow. The next thing I knew was a few minutes ago. By the way, what day is it?"

When Henri learned that he had been on the mountainside, unconscious, for three days, he was astounded. "So there is no chance now of catching Rancher," he remarked, disappointment in his voice.

The Danas' eyes lighted up and Louise said, "You won't believe this, but we think that

Rancher is in jail in Frankfurt. We believe he is a John Hudson from the United States."

"How astonishing!" Henri exclaimed.

Louise told how the prisoner had been captured after helping to steal important papers belonging to Rudolph. Then she briefly related the rest of the story.

Henri's eyes grew wide with amazement. "Rudolph!" he cried out. "Maybe Rudolph suffered a worse fate than I did at the hands of this fiend!"

The Danas had to admit that they were worried about Rudolph. But they tried to cheer Henri by suggesting that perhaps his brother was hiding from his enemies.

Henri shook his head sadly. "I am afraid that might not be so. Just before Rancher hit me, he said, 'Your brother is going to get the same kind of treatment, and then the Krisler heirlooms will be Franz's and mine!'"

There was silence for several minutes in the little chalet bedroom. The color drained from Henri's face and Frau Feer sprang forward. "You must rest. Please lie down," she urged.

But Henri waved her aside. "Do not worry about me," he begged. "This news about Rudolph will spur me on to regain my strength so I can find him."

The girls, nevertheless, felt that Henri should not talk any more and quietly excused themselves.

But Louise offered to telephone the Frankfurt *polizeiamt* at once for the latest information on the case, hoping that there might be some news of Rudolph.

"Our telephone is not working just now," said Frau Feer. "I expect the man to come and fix it soon, though."

Jean, who had noticed a small car standing in the roadway beside the chalet, suggested that she borrow it to run down to the hotel and make the telephone call from there.

Henri urged her to do so. "Frau Feer, give Jean the key. It's in my chest."

"I'll go with you," Doris said.

After the others left, Louise and Evelyn suggested that they go into the living room so Henri might rest, but he preferred to talk about the missing Krisler heirlooms. He asked Louise if she had picked up any clues. She opened Jean's bag and took out the paper which might be a copy of a map.

"Do you think," Evelyn asked, "that it's pointing out some hiding places in this chalet?"

Louise smiled. "That's a good guess, Ev. With Henri's permission we might start a search at once."

The permission was quickly granted, but Henri thoughtfully remarked that the girls had had a strenuous day and perhaps they would like to rest.

"Oh, no!" they said in unison.

Henri smiled. "Then please start the search. But I must warn you. The Feers, Rudolph, and I have already looked in all the usual hiding places. I wish you luck!"

Louise planted herself in the center of the living room and looked around, trying to decide where to start. Finally she decided to look for a possible secret compartment in the cupboards. Opening the wide, hand-carved doors of the dish cabinet, she began taking out cups, saucers, and plates.

"I'll help you," Evelyn said, and soon the cupboard was empty.

Louise began tapping the ceiling and side walls of the cabinet. But as she moved her knuckles from place to place there was no change in sound to indicate a hollow partition in back. Finally there was only the flooring of the cabinet left to test. Here the sound was different.

"There might be something here!" Louise exclaimed excitedly.

Evelyn watched intently as Louise pushed and hammered on the board with her fists. Deciding that more pressure might be needed, Louise asked Evelyn to assist her. Together the two girls leaned with the full weight of their arms and shoulders on one end of the flooring. It creaked!

"The shelf's moving!" Evelyn cried out.

A moment later the board tilted upward. Eagerly Louise peered beneath the upended section.

CHAPTER IX

A Worrisome Wait

"EVELYN, I see something underneath!" Louise cried gleefully. "Go see if Henri is well enough to get out of bed and take a look!"

Though extremely curious to know what the object was, Louise waited for the others. In a few moments, Henri, clad in bathrobe and slippers, joined the girls. His face was flushed with excitement. "You've found an heirloom?" he asked eagerly, as the Feers joined the group.

"There's something in this space under the bottom shelf," Louise replied. "It may be one of your heirlooms. In any case, I think you should be the one to find it."

Henri's long, slender fingers, trembling a bit, reached into the dark space. As he felt around, his eyes lighted up. A moment later he drew forth a large silver shield. The heavily embossed piece of metal was badly tarnished, but otherwise it was in excellent condition.

"The Krisler family shield!" Henri burst out. He gazed at it with loving eyes, then said, "Louise, I feel sure now that our family heirlooms have not been stolen. Those dear old servants of ours, Anna and Fritz, probably hid them well."

Frau Feer offered to polish the shield at once, so they might all enjoy its beauty. While she was in the kitchen doing this, Henri investigated the secret compartment, but no other heirlooms came to light. Henri said he was feeling much stronger, and wanted to help the girls in a further search.

"First," Louise spoke up, "I'd like to ask you a very pointed question if I may."

"Go right ahead," Henri said.

Louise asked for full details of his cousin Hermann Krisler. At once Henri's face clouded over. "My brother and I do not have a very high opinion of him. He is the black sheep of the Krisler family."

Henri stared at the floor for several seconds before going on. "Hermann claims that he has a half interest in the missing heirlooms. Rudolph and I do not believe this, but the records have been lost. My brother has been traveling a great deal lately trying to find the lost proof. We think the things came down through our mother's family but we have not been able to establish this."

Henri requested that the girls tell him how they had met Hermann, and what they knew about him. After learning the story, he remarked, "I am afraid he is here in Grindelwald to make trouble. I doubt that he was on his way up the mountain to rescue me. More likely he was going to threaten me."

Just then, Frau Feer walked in from the kitchen with the gleaming shield.

A majestic lion was embossed in the center, his head craned toward birds in a tree. The three other corners contained a crown, a castle, and a lily. Across the bottom was an inscription which Henri translated. It said: *"In battle or in peace, God leads us on."*

"Didn't you say this is a Krisler shield?" Evelyn asked.

"Yes, it is," Henri answered. "But we think all the other heirlooms of gold, silver, and jewels, came down through my mother's family." As a car roared up to the doorway and stopped, he said, "Your friends must be back."

Jean and Doris hurried into the chalet. "Good news!" Jean announced. "Henri, your brother Rudolph is safe!"

"Thank goodness!" Henri exclaimed happily.

Jean said that although the Frankfurt police had learned this much information from a restaurant owner, they still had not found out where the prince was staying.

"That does not matter, so long as he is all right," Henri said. "It is just possible he will come here. I certainly hope so, now that you have started to locate the heirlooms." He pointed to the beautiful shield.

Jean and Doris gasped in amazement when they heard about its hiding place, then both girls went over to look beneath the shelf.

"Very clever," Doris remarked. "But no more hunting without me. I want to be here the next time something is uncovered."

"We'll continue tomorrow, if it's all right with you," Louise said to Henri.

The young man frowned slightly. "I was hoping— Oh, please go on with your sleuthing now— that is, unless you are too weary."

The girls insisted that they were not, and Jean said that Aunt Harriet, knowing the girls were safe at the chalet, was not expecting them back for supper at any particular time.

"Then we'll work a little longer," Louise decided. Turning to her sister, she said laughingly, "It's your turn, Jean. See if you can uncover something. Henri, can you suggest an object for her to find?"

The guide's eyes twinkled. "One of the pieces I always liked was brought out at Christmas time. It was a wassail bowl."

"You once told us about a silver peacock," Frau Feer spoke up.

"And some fine old swords," her husband reminded Henri. "You said several of your family were knights during the Crusades."

"Yes, that is true," said the young man. He looked very sober. "Those wars were more glamorous than the ones of the past hundred years, but all war is bad." Then he threw off the momentary serious mood. Laughing, he said, "Jean, find me a box of jewels and I'll give you one from it!"

"That's a real challenge. Here I go!" said Jean, grinning.

After looking around the living room for a few seconds, she decided to investigate the beamed ceiling, and asked for a stepladder. When Herr Feer produced one, she climbed up.

One by one, Jean tapped the beams, climbing up and down the ladder to reach each one. When all but the last had been investigated, she sighed. "Apparently these beams are all solid and are part of the house construction," she remarked. "No chance for anything to be secreted inside them."

Without much hope, she mounted the ladder for the last time to tap a short section of beam which ran above an alcove between the fireplace and the door to the kitchen.

"Say," she said excitedly, "this seems to be different! It sounds as if it is hollow!"

Coming down the ladder, she asked Evelyn to go up and test it. Evelyn reached the same conclusion. "But how are you going to find out?" she asked, descending the ladder. "That beam looks as if it has been wedged in there a long time."

Jean was already quickly climbing the ladder.

She began tugging at one end of the beam. At first her efforts were fruitless, then suddenly she felt the wood give a bit.

"It's coming!" she exclaimed.

"Be careful!" Louise warned her.

Jean was too intent on her tugging to pay attention. She had just about concluded that she would need tools to pry out the beam when suddenly it gave way, throwing her off balance.

The ladder tilted, and the heavy beam fell toward Jean!

Almost at the same moment, Henri sprang forward, caught Jean, and yanked her out of the way. The beam barely missed her as it crashed to the floor!

When Jean recovered from her fright, she smiled at Henri. "I guess we've evened the score now on saving lives. Thanks."

There was no doubt but that the beam was hollow. Curious to know what might be inside, the group decided that tools should be brought at once. Herr Feer hurried to his workshop and brought back a kit. Jean was just selecting a chisel from it, when Frau Feer, looking from the window, cried out:

"*Hier kommt Hermann Krisler!* Your cousin is coming, Henri!"

"Oh, he must not learn our secret!" Henri exclaimed. "We must put everything away before he gets here!"

As if there had been a previous rehearsal, the group jumped to perform various tasks. Doris put the shield back in its hiding place and slammed down the shelf. Evelyn began restoring the dishes to the cupboard with furious energy.

The stepladder had been righted and Henri was now on top of it. Herr Feer held up one end of the beam, Louise and Jean the other.

"Hurry!" Frau Feer called. "Hermann is almost here!" But it was doubtful that the ceiling beam could be replaced in time.

Suddenly Louise called out, "Doris, run outside and stall Hermann as long as you can!"

CHAPTER X

Thief in Disguise

As Doris hurried outdoors, Frau Feer pulled a table over near the stepladder and climbed on top of it. With her added assistance and a hammer from the tool kit, the ceiling beam was wedged back into place.

"Whew!" said Louise, flopping into a rocking chair.

Frau Feer climbed down from her perch and dragged the table into place. Her husband took the stepladder into the kitchen and Evelyn quickly brushed the floor where dust had fallen when the old beam crashed.

Henri asked the girls not to tell his cousin Hermann about his adventure on the mountainside, then he went to his bedroom to put on his shirt and trousers. He was just emerging when Doris and Hermann walked in.

"*Ach!*" he exclaimed, upon seeing Henri. "You

are here! These people told me you must have had an accident on the mountain."

"There are always accidents," Henri replied noncommittally, and did not explain further.

"I guess you know why I am here," said Hermann, seating himself and facing the group. "There has been enough time wasted over the Krisler heirlooms. I want my share and I intend to have it."

"Have you any suggestions where they are?" Henri asked him icily.

Hermann said that he had a very definite idea Rudolph and Henri knew where the heirlooms were hidden—or, at least, had a clue but were not divulging it. "You have kept me waiting long enough," he said menacingly, wagging a finger at his cousin.

The girls were embarrassed. Following Louise's lead, they all stood up.

"We must leave now," said Louise and added, hoping to throw Hermann Krisler off the scent, "We'll see all of you in a couple of days. We girls are going on a sight-seeing trip."

Henri smiled at them gratefully. He understood what Louise was trying to do. Aloud, he merely said, "Come to see us when you return."

The girls said good-by to everyone and set off for the hotel. When they reached the roadway, Evelyn burst out, "That man Hermann! I can't stand him! I hope he won't force Henri into revealing any secrets."

"I don't think you need worry about that," Jean said with a laugh. "Do you suppose he has any connection with the smugglers? With all the excitement the past few days, we haven't had time to uncover any more clues in that department."

"True," said Louise. "But we can only do one thing at a time."

Aunt Harriet was exceedingly glad to see the girls. "It's been a long day without you. I want to hear all about everything."

Her nieces and their friends quickly took baths, changed their clothes, and then joined her for a late supper in the dining room.

After receiving a full account of the day's activities, Aunt Harriet remarked with a sigh, "Well, I'm certainly glad you're all here in one piece. I don't know that you should continue trying to solve this mystery if it's going to involve such hazardous work."

Jean leaned across the table and patted her aunt's hand. "Please don't worry, Aunty dear. You know we're pretty sturdy girls."

"I know, and smart too, but there's always a first time," Aunt Harriet protested. "I suppose there's no stopping you now, but I beg you please be careful."

Louise suggested that they spend the next couple of days with her just sight-seeing. "We'll have a wonderful time. First stop Interlaken. I hear there is to be a festival there tomorrow."

"That should be very interesting," Aunt Harriet said, "and colorful too. The hotel manager has been telling me about it. There will be dancers from the different cantons of Switzerland in their native costumes and a flag-tossing exhibition."

"And don't forget the men who blow those enormous Alpine horns," Doris spoke up.

The group, looking forward eagerly to the next day's trip, decided to retire early. As they walked through the lobby, Aunt Harriet and the girls stopped to speak to the hotel manager and arrange to rent a car for the drive to Interlaken.

"Are you having a good time?" he asked.

"Yes, indeed," Jean answered. "We're looking forward to exploring the country around here."

"I have a suggestion," the manager said. "There is a very charming private restaurant on the road to Lucerne from Interlaken. It is run by people named Kunkel. I will give you a card of introduction. Should you want to go there, just present it and you'll have one of the finest meals in all of Switzerland."

"Thank you, we'd love to do that," said Aunt Harriet.

She and the girls waited while the hotel mana-

ger went into his office to get the card. As Aunt
Harriet put it into her purse, the manager told her
he would telephone the Kunkels to expect her and
the girls the next day. Then the group said good
night and started upstairs.

"Hi, girls!" called a voice behind them.

Turning, they were confronted by Fred Cox.
Not far behind him were his parents. All were
grinning widely at the Dana group.

"I see you got back all right," said Fred cheerily.

"And no thanks to you," said Doris tartly.

"Oh, come now, don't be so hard on me," Fred
pleaded. "You don't look pretty when you pout.
Tell me, did you find Henri?"

Louise answered in an even voice, "Henri is at
home."

Fred Cox apparently realized that he was going
to get no further information, so he did not pursue
the subject. Instead he asked, "Say, Doris, what
are you doing tomorrow? Now don't tell me
you're going to be busy. The folks and I are going
to Lucerne. I'd love to have you come along."

"Thank you, but I have other plans," Doris told
him.

Fred shrugged. "Have it your own way," he
said.

Doris said good night and the others nodded,
then all went upstairs to their rooms. Before
climbing into bed, Doris and Evelyn came into the

room occupied by Aunt Harriet and her nieces. The conversation turned to the Coxes.

"They're impossible!" Doris said.

Aunt Harriet told the girls that the day before their substitute chambermaid had talked to her about them. She had tried to avoid the gossipy woman, but found it impossible. According to the maid, the Coxes had a very large collection of carved wooden bottle stoppers in their rooms.

"Whatever are they going to do with them all?" Evelyn asked.

"The chambermaid said she heard Mr. Cox say he was taking them to everybody in the firm where he works. Mrs. Cox and Fred are going to give them to all their friends and relatives too. But this is the surprising part of the chambermaid's story—for themselves they're buying some attractive jewelry."

The girls giggled and Doris remarked, "Sounds just like them. Selfish as can be!"

After breakfast the next morning the group went out to the hotel driveway. Parked there was the small car which Louise had arranged with the hotel manager to rent.

"We can't all get in that!" Evelyn exclaimed as she eyed the tiny automobile.

"Oh, yes, we can. The manager assured me that it would seat five," Louise answered.

Giggling, the other three girls crowded into the

back seat. Louise slipped behind the wheel and Aunt Harriet sat beside her.

When they reached Interlaken, the town was in a gay holiday mood. The colorful folk entertainment had already started in the park.

Louise, who was looking for a place to park the car, suddenly exclaimed, "I just saw a man who looked like Mr. Cox go into that big hotel."

"But Mr. Cox was going to Lucerne, wasn't he?" Aunt Harriet asked.

Louise smiled. "Not only that, but this man had a mustache, so I guess I was wrong."

"What's more," said Doris, "Fred invited me to go to Lucerne with the three of them, so it couldn't have been Mr. Cox."

The car was parked and the girls walked to the scene of the festival. At the edge of the grassy area were tables with red-and-white cloths and over some were large colored umbrellas. In the distance loomed the majestic Jungfrau.

The Danas found a large table and seated themselves. When a waitress came, they all ordered Swiss milk drinks, but were so fascinated by the entertainment they hardly paid attention to the tall glasses which were set in front of them.

Groups of eight, consisting of four girls and four men, formed for the folk dances. In one group the girls wore elaborate headdresses of black-and-white pleated lace, with a red ribbon hanging down the back. Wide white collars and cuffs of the same lace trimmed their black dresses.

A woman at the next table said to the Americans, "These dancers came from Appenzell, a town famous for its needlework."

In the next group the girls' costumes consisted of black skirts, white blouses with fluted sleeves, and sleeveless red jackets. The men wore black velvet jackets and small yellow-and-black caps perched jauntily on the backs of their heads.

The band struck up a gay tune and the dancing began. Back and forth and in and out they went, performing the intricate figures of the folk dances.

Suddenly the Danas' attention was attracted to a man who came running across the road from the big hotel. He was waving his arms and crying out, first in German, then in English, "I have been robbed! My jewelry shop in the hotel has been robbed! By a man with a black mustache! Has anyone seen a man with a black mustache?"

The girls were electrified. The man with the mustache whom Louise had noticed going into the hotel must have been the thief! She said to the distressed jeweler, "I think I saw him a little while ago. He was wearing a dark suit." When the jeweler nodded, she said, "I'll keep a lookout, and if I find him, I'll report it to the police."

"Oh, thank you," the man said, and hurried on his way.

"I wonder what the thief took," said Jean, as

she turned back to watch the next performers.

Three men in black velvet shorts, white soft shirts, and embroidered jackets walked onto the field. As the band played, the men began to toss the bright-red flags with the white cross in the center. In time to the music, the flags soared up and were expertly caught when they came down.

"Aren't those men marvelous!" Jean exclaimed. "They never drop a flag."

"They're like our drum majors at home," Doris agreed. "They never drop a baton."

The flag tossing was followed by the Alpine horn blowing. The girls were amazed at the mellow tones which came from the extremely long wooden horns.

The woman at the next table leaned over to say, "It's almost unbelievable, but the sound will carry six miles."

When the entertainment was over, Aunt Harriet announced that she would like to walk around the town and do a little shopping. As they strolled across the street toward the hotel where the jewelry store had been robbed, Jean suddenly leaned down and said, "Well, what do you know about this?" She straightened up. Between her fingers dangled a false black mustache!

"The thief!" Louise cried out. "He must have dropped it."

Aunt Harriet and the other girls were inclined to agree. They decided to show it to the jeweler.

He proved to be the clerk from whom the mysterious stranger had stolen two very valuable watches while purchasing a third.

"Yes, this looks like his mustache," the clerk said excitedly. He called the manager and a discussion followed. The police were summoned for

"I have been robbed!" the man cried out.

a second time and thanked the Danas for their helpfulness.

Louise made no mention of the similarity in appearance between the thief and Mr. Cox. But it went through her mind that it was a good thing Mr. Cox had an alibi. He could pass for the thief's twin brother!

"It would be mighty embarrassing to be mistaken for a thief," she thought.

Before leaving the shop, Aunt Harriet and Doris each bought attractive silver pins with the Swiss national flower embossed on them. Finally the tourists went to their car and started for the Kunkel restaurant.

Several miles out of town, in the direction of Lucerne, Louise slowed down because of a truck ahead. It was small and apparently not too powerful, for it was crawling up the incline.

The rear of the truck was square and high slats went around three sides. Inside the enclosure was an enormous circular, cheesecloth-wrapped object.

"What in the world is that?" Evelyn asked.

"My guess is that it's a cheese," Aunt Harriet told her. "A Swiss farmer delivers his cheese to market this way. They are very heavy. I should say this one weighs as much as ninety pounds."

Miss Dana went on to explain that it took weeks, even months, for a farmer to produce a wheel of cheese this size and it provided his livelihood for some time to come. "I've read that—"

She was interrupted by a scream from Doris. "Look out!"

The tail gate of the truck had jarred open. The huge cheese bounced out and landed on its rim in the roadway. It began to roll toward the Dana car!

Louise quickly twisted the steering wheel to the left, to avoid hitting the tremendous mass of cheese. But a car coming from the opposite direction prevented her turning in. She did not dare pull off the road to the right because there was a sheer drop at that side.

Louise held her breath, hoping the giant cheese would pass them. But suddenly the swiftly rolling wheel changed its course and smashed head on into the car!

CHAPTER XI

Obnoxious Tourists

THE IMPACT against the car jolted the passengers badly. When they recovered themselves, they realized that the great wheel of cheese had smashed one of the headlights. The cheesecloth had burst and yellowish white blobs had spattered all over the windshield and hood.

"Ugh! What a mess!" Doris called out.

"It sure is," said Jean. She chuckled. "I'm glad that whole cheese didn't hit me!"

By this time the farmer had climbed down from his truck. He walked back to survey the damage and the Dana group could hear him jabbering volubly in German.

Louise stepped from the car, followed by the others. "Do you speak English?" she asked the man.

"*Ach, ja,*" the farmer replied. "I make much trouble for you. I must pay what I hurt you. For me—the big work of my summer is gone!"

Aunt Harriet and the girls felt very sorry for the farmer. Despite the fact that he was inadvertently responsible for the accident, their only thought was to help him.

Suddenly Louise had an idea. She dipped her finger into a part of the untouched cheese and popped a large piece of it into her mouth. "Um," she said, "this is good. Taste it, girls."

All the others, including Aunt Harriet, scooped out pieces of the delicious cheese. Louise asked the man what kind it was.

"Emmentaler," he said proudly.

Louise asked him how much a ten-pound Emmentaler cheese would cost.

The farmer looked at her in amazement. "You want me to give you ten pounds of this cheese to pay for the broken headlight?" he asked.

Louise grinned. "I might do better than that. I might buy some. How would you like to send a ten-pound cheese to each of our homes?" Before the startled farmer could reply, Louise turned to Jean. "How about you and me sending one to Ken and Chris, too. We had that thought in mind. Remember?"

"Indeed I do, and I think it's a neat idea," Jean answered. "Ever since the boys sent us those gorgeous going-away orchids I've wanted to do something for them."

In reply to Louise's questions, the farmer said that he had made some small cheeses which he had planned to keep for his own use, but he would be glad to let the girls have them. In the end, six ten-pound Emmentaler cheeses were ordered. One was to go to Uncle Ned Dana on the *Balaska*, another would be sent to Starhurst School where the girls might enjoy it with their friends.

Another would go to the Dana home in Oak Falls, one to Doris's parents, one to Evelyn's brother, and the last to Ken and Chris. The farmer insisted upon giving them a special price. The difference between the price the farmer usually charged and the sum at which he would sell the six to the girls would pay for the damage to the rented car.

"You are very kind Americans," the man said. "May God bless you all!"

Then he took several rags from his truck and wiped off the car as best he could. With the girls' help, the battered wheel of cheese was lifted back into his truck and the tail gate securely fastened. The Dana party said good-by to him and Louise drove off.

A few miles farther on they came to a garage and Louise drove in to get a new headlight. "Let's not bother about other repairs until after we turn the car in at Grindelwald," she suggested.

It was late afternoon when they arrived at the Kunkel home. The private restaurant was one of the most attractive chalets the travelers had seen. It was three stories high and had many leaded-glass windows. The upper part of the house was carved in floral designs, and the rose-and-gentian pattern under the long gable was painted in soft hues of rose and blue. Tall rhododendron bushes bloomed in profusion. Beyond sparkled the bluish water of the Lake of Brienz.

"Somebody else is here to eat," Doris remarked, nodding toward a parked car.

Aunt Harriet gave an involuntary sigh of annoyance "I'm sorry to have to tell you girls this, but that car is the one I've seen the Coxes driving."

"Oh, no!" Doris groaned. "Louise, drive on."

"And miss a meal that's out of this world?" said Jean. "Nothing doing!"

Louise parked and Aunt Harriet and the girls went up the long stairway. Their knock was answered by a pretty, gray-haired woman. She was short, rather stout, and had delightful laughter lines creasing her face. Aunt Harriet presented the card of introduction and Mrs. Kunkel invited them inside.

"I am very happy that you came," she said. "You understand that practically everything is cooked to order, so there will be a wait."

"Yes, we were told that," Aunt Harriet replied.

Their hostess led the way into a large adjoining room. "We have other guests," she said.

"Hi!" Fred Cox said, getting up and bounding across the room. He turned to Mrs. Kunkel. "No introductions necessary. We're old buddies."

"Sure," added Mr. Cox, also getting up and directing Aunt Harriet to a seat beside his wife. Louise, noting that he wore a light suit, concluded that he could not possibly have been the man she had seen in Interlaken.

The girls tried to take chairs together to avoid the two men, but Fred elbowed his way in between Doris and Louise, while his father sat between the other two girls.

"Well, what did you think of the Interlaken Festival?" Fred asked. "A big bore, isn't it?"

"We enjoyed everything very much," said Doris stiffly. "It was beautiful, wasn't it, girls?"

Mr. Cox laughed uproariously. "You folks amaze me. I thought all that women liked to do was shop. Now take my wife here. A whole day in Lucerne to sight-see and all she wanted to do was buy a watch!"

"Why, Al*bert!*"—Mrs. Cox giggled—"you told me before we made this trip that I might pick out a beautiful watch." She arose and came over toward the girls. Pulling up her left sleeve, she showed them a tiny watch, its face surrounded by diamonds.

"How gorgeous!" Evelyn exclaimed.

"It put me back plenty," said Mr. Cox. He reached into his pocket and pulled out a bill of sale from one of Lucerne's leading jewelry shops. "Look at that!" he said. "Or can't you read this gibberish in francs? Well, I'll tell you. That means in good old American money two hundred dollars."

Jean glanced quickly at the sheet. She noticed the purchase of two other watches on it. Apparently Mr. Cox read her thoughts and said, "Fred and I each got a beauty too." Both men displayed gleaming and attractive new wrist watches.

At once the Dana girls recalled the mustached man in Interlaken. If Mr. Cox should need an alibi to prove that he had been in Lucerne, he was holding it in his hand!

Mrs. Cox inquired whether the Danas had made any purchases that day. To be sociable, Aunt Harriet and Doris opened their purses and showed the pins they had bought. The other girls could see that Mrs. Cox was not impressed, probably classifying the purchases as cheap trinkets.

But her husband asked, "I suppose you got a sales slip?"

"Why, no," Aunt Harriet replied. "These didn't cost very much."

"Nevertheless," said Mr. Cox firmly, "you should get a sales slip for everything you buy in Europe. You need them to show to the customs authorities in New York."

"Thank you for warning us," said Aunt Harriet. "We'll do that in the future."

Presently the conversation turned to the theft

of jewelry from Mrs. Cox at the hotel. Her face clouded and she fumed over the inefficiency of the Swiss police.

This was too much for Jean. "I've always understood that they were among the finest police in the world," she said.

Louise brought up the subject of the porcelain cow, but the Coxes had nothing new to offer on this subject.

"Why discuss that?" Fred spoke up. "You'll probably never find out who threw it. Say, how about a little entertainment while we're waiting?"

The girls groaned inwardly. Was this pest going to sing again? Their eyes followed him as he arose and walked over to the corner of the room. For the first time they noticed an accordian.

"Oh, no, he isn't going to—!" Doris thought wildly.

Fred Cox picked up the highly polished, black accordian with a gleaming ivory keyboard and silver stops. After adjusting the leather straps over his shoulders, he slipped his left hand under the band and pulled the instrument out full length. As he squeezed it together with an earsplitting discord, he laughed and asked:

"Well, how about some Swiss tunes á la Américain?"

Without waiting for an answer he began jazzing a native melody, singing it partly in English and partly in German. The whole effect was ludicrous.

Aunt Harriet looked at him disapprovingly. "I am sure that the feelings of our host and hostess will be hurt," she said.

"*Ach, ja?*" Fred said. "What does it matter? We're paying plenty for a good dinner, and if it isn't ready, what are we supposed to do? Sit around here like mummies?"

Aunt Harriet's prediction was true. A few moments later a fine-looking, white-haired man appeared in the doorway. He bowed to the Dana group and said, "Mama and I appreciate your coming." Then he strode over to Fred Cox and took the accordian away from him. "If you want music, I will play it for you."

Herr Kunkel proved to be an excellent musician. His fingers flew over the keyboard with speed and accuracy. His repertoire was large; he played not only well-known Swiss airs, but arias from operas, and finally some popular American musical-comedy numbers. When he finished, his audience clapped loudly.

"And now," said Frau Kunkel from the doorway, "will you all please come to dinner? I have prepared *koenigsberger klops* for you. I hope you will enjoy it."

The Americans certainly did enjoy it! Aunt Harriet inquired what the ingredients were, and was told that the recipe included ground pork, ground veal, eggs, milk, slices of bread, vinegar, salt and pepper, butter, flour, capers, and several cups of meat stock.

"It's simply delectable," Doris raved.

With the *koenigsberger klop*, their hostess served Swiss pear bread. This, she told them, was made by mixing dried prunes and pears with the dough, raisins, currants, citron, orange and lemon peel, together with cinnamon, cloves, and anise. To the whole was added four cups of fruit juice.

"Oh, Aunt Harriet," said Jean enthusiastically, "let's take the recipes home."

Mrs. Kunkel smiled in a pleasant way, then she said, "And perhaps you would like to take my recipe for cheesecake too. I will serve that for dessert." After her guests had eaten the cheesecake, all of them asked for the recipe.

Herr Kunkel laughed. "I tell Mama she should not give away all her secrets. Then nobody will come here to eat." He smiled affectionately at his wife and added, "But I should not worry. Mama has that special little touch which makes her cooking taste better than anyone else's who uses the recipes!"

When the diners left the table, they returned to the spacious living room. Fred called Doris over to a window, to see the view. Mrs. Cox sat down and picked up a book with photographs of Switzerland, while Mr. Cox paced up and down the long room humming off key.

"Oh, why are those awful people sticking around?" Jean asked in exasperation.

"I suggest that we stay until they've left," Louise said. "I'd like to get better acquainted with the Kunkels."

"So would I," her sister agreed.

But the Coxes showed no signs of leaving and finally Louise went into the kitchen to speak to Mrs. Kunkel. "We have been hoping your other guests might leave," she told the woman. "My sister and I would like to visit with you and your husband."

"We, too, would be happy if they would go," Mrs. Kunkel replied. "It is fortunate for your country that not many of your citizens are like the Coxes."

The woman smiled. "From what the hotel manager said on the phone, I know you girls like adventure. I have something to suggest. Our son Edouard owns a small plane and does rescue work, even in the deepest snows. How would you like to go with him to see the world's most famous avalanche dogs?"

CHAPTER XII

Avalanche Dogs

"The trip sounds wonderful, Frau Kunkel," said Louise. "But what are avalanche dogs?"

"Do you know the St. Bernard breed?" asked the Swiss woman kindly. She explained that the term "avalanche dogs" was just another name for the famous St. Bernards who went on rescue missions.

"Oh, you mean the dogs trained at the St. Bernard Hospice," Louise said excitedly. "I remember reading about them back in school in the United States."

Frau Kunkel nodded. "I suggest that you and your friends stay here all night. My son is coming and I am sure he has no engagements for tomorrow. He often takes tourists on flights over the Alps. Would you like to go?"

The woman went on to say that the plane was a small four-passenger craft and he could take only two of the girls at a time. "So you will have to take turns. But it is not very far to the Hospice, and there will be plenty of time for all of you to make the trip tomorrow—two in the morning and two in the afternoon."

Louise was thrilled by the idea of going on such an exciting trip. "You are wonderful to suggest such an interesting flight, Frau Kunkel."

Then Louise became serious. "But we must not let the Coxes hear about this. They will certainly want to go, and this is one trip I would like to take without being bothered by Fred and his parents and their silly conversation." She giggled and whispered in Frau Kunkel's ear, "You will have to help me get rid of them!"

The woman smiled knowingly. "I have a plan in mind if your aunt will co-operate."

"Oh, I know she will," Louise said quickly.

"Good! You tell Miss Dana to pretend she is not feeling well when I give the signal. I think the scheme will work," Frau Kunkel explained.

Louise returned to the living room, where she found Fred Cox trying to persuade Doris to ride back with him and his parents.

"Oh, please, Fred," Doris replied, "I want to stay with my friends. I'll see you in the morning."

A look of annoyed amusement came over Fred's face. "It won't work, young lady. You've put me off too many times already. You and I are going to have a date and that's all there is to it!"

Aunt Harriet, seated in the corner of the room

away from Fred and Doris, frowned. She had said nothing up to this point about Fred's unwelcome attentions. She was about to speak her mind, however, when Louise leaned over and said in a low voice:

"Aunt Harriet, there's a wonderful plan afoot. It means our staying here all night. But you'll have to pretend to be ill when Frau Kunkel suggests it."

"But I—" Aunt Harriet started to say, then caught herself. "All right, dear."

The argument between Doris and Fred was becoming heated and unpleasant when Frau Kunkel came into the room. "Why, Miss Dana," she said in a loud voice which drowned Fred Cox's, "how pale you are! Don't you feel well? I hope my cooking—"

Aunt Harriet put her hand to her forehead. "I— I—think I *would* like to lie down," she said.

With Frau Kunkel and Louise helping her, Aunt Harriet was led to a first-floor bedroom. When they reached it, the door was closed and Louise and the two women giggled. An instant later the door opened. Jean, Evelyn, and Doris rushed in.

"Close the door! Quick!" Louise ordered. Then in a whisper she told about the ruse and the wonderful plans for the next day.

There was a knock on the door. Jean opened it

to find Herr Kunkel standing there. "Is Miss Dana very ill?" he asked worriedly.

Quickly Jean explained the situation, and the man burst into laughter. "You need have no more fears. Your friends have left. The minute they sensed trouble, they decided to run!"

"Well, I hope this is the end of Fred trying to date me," Doris sighed, then giggled. "Thanks, everybody."

A short time later Edouard Kunkel came home. He was a tall, good-looking young man, with a good-natured expression. He gladly assented to the trip the next day and suggested they leave early.

Three third-floor bedrooms were assigned to the Dana group. The charming, well-furnished quarters contained high, double feather beds. On them lay long muslin nightgowns trimmed with handmade lace. The girls climbed into the soft beds wondering if they would be able to sleep on feathers. But after what seemed only a few minutes it was morning and someone was knocking on the doors.

"Good morning!" called Louise, the first one awake. "We'll get right up and be downstairs in a jiffy."

It was decided that she and Jean should be Edouard's first passengers. As soon as breakfast was over, he led the sisters outside. To their amazement, they found a long runway back of the house and his small plane at one end of it.

As the girls drew nearer they could see skis between the front wheels of the plane. Edouard explained that they were worked by hydraulic lift.

"I leave these skis on all the time, even in summer," he explained. "I get calls for rescue work up in the snowy areas all year round."

The Danas took seats behind the pilot and soon they were soaring over an entrancing panorama. Green, brown, and white formed a patchwork pattern. The flight southwestward to the St. Bernard Hospice did not take long. As the plane hovered over the large, impressive buildings of the monastery set among the rocky crags, the girls noticed the long ribbon of road that led up the mountainside to it.

"With luck, I'll come down on that road," said Edouard. The girls knew from his grin that he was only joking.

As they expected, he circled the area several times, then made a perfect landing. Edouard and the girls climbed out and walked toward the towering monastery and adjoining hotel. Presently a smiling, deeply sun-tanned monk about thirty years old came out to greet them. He wore a long black cassock, tied at the waist with a fringed sash. On his head was a wide-brimmed black felt hat with a low, rounded crown.

"Good morning, Father Rusko," said Edouard.

"May I introduce my American friends, Louise and Jean Dana? With your permission, Father, the girls would like to see the St. Bernard dogs."

"I will be glad to show them to you," said the monk. He led the way to a long, low stone building some hundred yards distant. "Listen!"

The great dogs began barking, but when Father Rusko led the way inside the building, they became quiet and sat down facing the visitors.

"They're beautiful!" Louise exclaimed. "And so big and majestic. How much do they weigh?"

"Around a hundred and fifty pounds each," Father Rusko replied.

"They're lovely," Jean remarked, "but they look so mournful."

"Yes, they do," Father Rusko said. "But actually they are not. The St. Bernards are happy dogs and very friendly."

As if to prove the monk's words, one of the dogs suddenly bounded toward Louise, plunked his two front paws on her chest and knocked the girl over! As she sat down unexpectedly, the dog began to lick her face as if he were contrite.

"Why, Barry!" Father Rusko scolded. He then explained that this dog held the record for more rescues than any of the others. "He's amazing—he can scent a man, no matter how deeply he may be buried under a snowslide. Note his paws."

As the Danas looked at the enormous paws, Father Rusko went on, "You know, the St. Bernard literally 'swims' through the snow. These paws come in mighty handy."

"I've always understood," said Jean, "that when these dogs go out on a rescue mission they carry little casks on their collars so that the victim can have a stimulant."

The monk smiled. "Actually, that is not true. But to please tourists, we sometimes hang a cask on a dog's neck so they can take pictures." He gave a little chuckle, then said, "What is more important is that when the St. Bernard digs a victim out of the snow, he will keep licking the man's face until he awakens him. Then the dog will lie down beside the victim to keep him warm, and bark until we reach the man and carry him to the monastery."

Suddenly Jean's eyes lighted up. "Father Rusko, do you ever sell puppies?"

"Indeed we do," the monk replied. "Would you like one?"

Before replying, Jean looked at Louise. "Sis, don't you think it would be wonderful to have a St. Bernard dog at Starhurst School?"

"Oh, yes," Louise answered enthusiastically. Then she giggled and said, "Did you mean this as a gift to Professor and Mrs. Crandall?"

"I had something of the sort in mind," Jean confessed. "But the dog could be a pet of all the girls at school."

"And if the Crandalls didn't want him?" Louise suggested.

"Then Aunt Harriet could keep him for us at Oak Falls."

"Let's do it!" said Louise.

After receiving information on prices from Father Rusko, they ordered a puppy shipped to whichever address they should decide upon later. Jean said she would get in touch with Mrs. Crandall and ask her permission.

"It's time for the dogs to have their exercise," the monk said presently, opening the door and letting them run outside. "They must have regular periods each day to work off their energy," he explained. "This keeps them in good form."

Though the St. Bernards were large and heavy, they frisked about like puppies. "Oh, I'm so glad we decided to buy one," said Jean. "I can hardly wait to get it." She stood, fascinated, watching the big dogs race across the yard.

Their pilot, Edouard, suddenly looked up at the sky. Then he turned to Father Rusko. "*Foehn?*" he asked.

"I'm afraid so," the monk replied. "You'd better fly out of here fast while you can. You never know what these *foehns* may do."

Louise and Jean looked at each other. "I wonder what he means," Louise said in a low voice to her sister. "Edouard looks a little concerned. I hope it's nothing serious. He has the reputation of being a fine pilot, though, so we probably needn't worry."

The three visitors thanked Father Rusko for showing them the dogs, then hurried off to the plane. "I don't like a south wind in these mountains," Edouard said. "Climb in."

As soon as the three were seated in the plane, Edouard turned on the starter. There was no response. He tried again but no sound came from the engine. Louise and Jean looked at each other in concern.

CHAPTER XIII

A Clue Pays Off

THE DANA girls looked expectantly at the pilot. They almost wished now that the motor would not respond. If they should get into the air, and more trouble developed, it might be disastrous.

Edouard sat back in his bucket seat, checked the gauges on the panel in front of him, then reached forward and turned a switch, first to the right, then to the left. A second later the engine started, but almost immediately died.

The young Swiss smiled. "My mountain horse is a little balky." He turned the switch again and this time the motor started with a welcome roar, sending a cloud of fumes out the rear.

The girls marveled at the ease with which Edouard turned the plane around on the road, then went whizzing down it. In a few seconds they were air-borne. Louise and Jean looked down at the rugged scenery below them.

"I don't see any place to make an emergency landing," Jean whispered to her sister.

"Let's hope we won't have to," Louise replied.

But a few seconds later the engine sputtered and died. Louise and Jean clutched their seats. Edouard did not look worried. He glided gracefully, and then worked to restore power. The engine caught and they went on. There was no conversation, however, until they were nearing Interlaken.

Then Edouard said, "The motor will need a little work. It will be necessary for me to land at the Interlaken airfield. I am sorry, but I shall not be able to take your friends on the same trip today. Will you please phone the girls and tell them."

"Glad to," said Jean. "And we'll ask them to come and get us."

When the plane landed, the Danas thanked Edouard for the exciting trip, then hurried off to call the Kunkel home.

Aunt Harriet said that Doris and Evelyn had driven into town to do some more shopping. "If you look around town, I'm sure you'll see them," she told her nieces.

The girls caught a ride on a postal bus and soon were strolling down the main street of Interlaken.

"Here come Doris and Evelyn now," said Jean, looking ahead.

"And their arms are loaded with bundles," Louise remarked.

"But their purchases surely can't be as interest-

ing as ours," said Jean. "Wait until they hear about
the St. Bernard puppy!"

Doris and Evelyn were not only amazed and delighted to hear about the dog, but said they had
some news of their own. "We've been doing a
little sleuthing," said Evelyn proudly.

"Here in Interlaken?" Louise asked in surprise.

"Yes."

Evelyn said the girls had stopped at the hotel
jewelry shop to inquire if there were any news of
the thief. Learning there was none, the two girls
had decided to do some detective work.

"I really didn't think it would work," said Evelyn, "but I thought we might question some children. You know, there were a lot of them around
yesterday."

"That's right," Jean agreed. "Well, don't keep
us in suspense. What's the news?"

Doris, who said she was hungry, suggested that
they go into one of the hotels and have a snack
while they talked. When the four girls were
seated in the attractive coffee shop, decorated
with murals of the Alps, Evelyn began her story.
She said that while walking near the park, she and
Doris had stopped to watch a group of children.

"They were playing some kind of game which
we did not understand, but they were giggling
merrily. Suddenly a little boy ran from behind a
tree. He was wearing a mustache and as he
whipped past the others, he dropped it, and hur-

ried off. The other boys and girls doubled up with laughter."

Evelyn went on to say that she and Doris had become suspicious that the children might have been re-enacting a scene they had witnessed the day before. The thief wearing a false mustache had discarded it!

As she stopped speaking, Jean urged, "Go on! Then what did you do?"

"We spoke to the children, who were very friendly. They seemed anxious to practice their English. We asked them to repeat their little skit, and they were glad to do so. Then we asked what had made them think of it. As we suspected, they'd seen this very same thing happen the day before."

"You're wonderful!" said Jean. "Now we *know* that the thief discarded a false mustache!"

"And we found out something else," said Doris. "It sounds unbelievable, but here it is. It seems that as the mustached man was running away yesterday, the children were in his way. Some of them were seated in a circle on the ground, playing, and he stepped right among them."

Doris giggled and went on, "Those children had bright eyes. Two of them noticed that a small ball of twine the man dropped, but quickly picked up, was green and red."

"Well, that is a good clue," said Jean. "We

ought to add those children to Dana and Company, Detectives."

Louise asked whether Doris and Evelyn had reported their latest findings to the police. "We haven't had time yet," Evelyn admitted. "Let's go now."

As soon as the girls had finished their snack of chicken sandwiches and hot chocolate, they hurried off to police headquarters, where Evelyn and Doris reported the results of their detective work.

"And now, girls," said Louise, "I think we'd better drive to the Kunkels and pick up Aunt Harriet. I'd love to get back to the hotel, put on some fresh clothes, and start working on the mystery of the heirlooms. Oh, I hope Hermann has left the chalet!"

They walked to the car and in a short while were back at the Kunkel restaurant. Aunt Harriet was waiting for them, and after thanking Mrs. Kunkel for her hospitality, they set off for Grindelwald.

As they turned into the hotel driveway, they were stopped by Fred Cox. "Hi, Doris," he called out. "I saw you coming. Say, where were you last night?"

Before Doris could speak, Jean said quickly, "Goldilocks spent the night with the three bears. Next question?"

Fred Cox laughed. "So the detectives aren't going to tell where they were, eh?" When none of the girls answered, he said, "I've been waiting for the four of you. I thought maybe Doris would go some place with me if you all came along. So I'm inviting you now to go for a ride on the chair lift."

As Doris, Jean, and Evelyn in unison replied, "We can't—really we can't," Louise felt a little sorry for the young man. Smiling, she said, "Fred, I'm afraid you'd better give up trying to get us to do anything. We came to Switzerland with some pretty definite plans and we don't have much time to carry them out."

"What kind of plans?" the young man asked.

In reply, Louise said there were many places they wished to go and many people to see. Fred Cox, apparently realizing it was useless to prod the girls any more, turned on his heel abruptly, and left them.

Doris grabbed Louise's arm. "Oh, thanks a million."

The girls went to collect their mail and each received a couple of letters. The Danas had bulky envelopes from Chris and Ken.

Doris winked at Evelyn and said, "If those boys write such fat letters now, what size will they write when they receive that ten-pound cheese?"

Louise giggled. "I'll read Ken's letter later," she said. "I wonder who is writing to me from Frankfurt?"

The letter proved to be from the *wachtmeister*.

He stated that the police chief in Grindelwald had some interesting news for the Danas and suggested that they call on him.

"Oh, let's go see him right away!" Jean urged.

"Do you mind, Aunt Harriet?" Louise asked.

"No, dear. Go ahead."

The sisters hurried off. At police headquarters the officer in charge gave the young detectives a wide smile when they introduced themselves.

"The Frankfurt police want me to thank you for your work," he said. "You were very clever to prove that Rancher and Hudson were the same person by sending a sample of handwriting. The prisoner still denies any guilt, but Interpol has checked with the American police and they think this man may be a wanted smuggler."

"Then," said Lousie, "both he and Franz Dorfer are thieves and smugglers!"

"The police believe that is right," the officer told her. "And there's more good news. The *wachtmeister* said that Prince Rudolph had been in touch with the Frankfurt police. He had been held by Dorfer and Hudson and grueled about the family heirlooms. Rudolph had told them nothing, and later had managed to escape."

The Danas thanked him for the information and returned to the hotel. Aunt Harriet and the other two girls were excited to hear the latest developmen. When the babble died down, Aunt Harriet asked, "What's on your calendar for tomorrow?"

After a moment's thought Jean suggested that they telephone the Altberg Chalet at once and find out whether Hermann Krisler was still there. "If he is, let's go to church and Monday make the trip to the Jungfraujoch. But if he has left, I want to go to the chalet and continue our heirloom search. I'm dying to examine that hollow beam!"

She made the call and talked with Henri. He said that Hermann, outdoors at the moment, was still staying there and had been searching the chalet, but had found nothing. Jean thought she detected a note of relief in Henri's voice.

"I have more news for you about Rudolph!" Jean said. "We have just come back from a talk with the police chief in Grindelwald."

"Wonderful!" Henri exclaimed. "Where had he been?"

"I'll tell you all the details when I see you," Jean answered. "When do you think Hermann will be leaving the chalet?"

Henri sighed. "I hope it will be soon. I'd like you girls to come back and complete your search."

"We're enjoying our sight-seeing in the meantime," Jean told him. "Perhaps Monday we'll ride up on the train as far as it goes, and probably climb the rest of the Jungfrau from there."

"Promise me you will be careful," Henri pleaded.

Jean laughingly promised, then added, "I hope by the following day your cousin will be gone, so we girls can get to work. Good-by now."

"*Auf Wiedersehen*," Henri responded.

After supper the girls decided to take a short stroll in the beautiful moonlight. They walked to the edge of town, then started up the mountain road.

Suddenly Louise pointed up the mountainside. "There's a plane! Way up at the snow line!"

As the girls watched the small craft, distinct in the moonlight, it seemed to be heading straight into the mountain. "It's going to crash!" Doris cried out. "Oh, how dreadful! It did crash!"

CHAPTER XIV

A Dangerous Climb

THE GIRLS stood in horrified silence. Any plane crash was a sickening thought. But they were personally worried that the victim might be Edouard Kunkel.

"Oh, why did he have to fly up there at night?" Doris exclaimed.

Louise had already shaken off her momentary fright. Recalling that Edouard made rescue flights all the time, she said perhaps the pilot had not crashed—that he had landed safely.

"Well, we'll know in a few minutes," said Jean.

The eyes of the four girls did not leave the snowy mountain peak for ten minutes. Then, to their intense relief, they saw the plane take off, circle once, and head for Interlaken.

"Thank goodness!" said Evelyn, as the girls turned to go back to the hotel.

The next morning they heard from the manager

that it was indeed Edouard Kunkel who had made a daring rescue of a climber.

Since it was Sunday, the girls decided to spend a quiet day. After church services, they wrote long letters to their friends back home and then took Aunt Harriet for a drive.

"I suggest we all go to bed early this evening," Miss Dana said. "Our trip up the Jungfrau will make a long day tomorrow."

After an early breakfast Aunt Harriet and the girls started up the street for the railroad station. "You look very attractive," Miss Dana said to her companions.

Louise was wearing powder-blue ski pants; the other girls had on blue-black ones. All four girls carried extra sweaters to put on over their lighter-weight ones.

A large group of sight-seers boarded the train. With all the windows open and the sun streaming in, it climbed the mountain among the chalets and farms, myriads of flowers, and herds of cattle.

Finally the train reached a stop, Kleine Scheidegg. Here everyone alighted and walked around to admire the exquisite view. There were no trees at this height. But blue and yellow gentians, alpine roses and leopard's bane, orchids, and alpine asters grew in profusion. Far below, surrounded by fruit orchards, was the village of Grindelwald. In contrast, snow-clad mountains rose to left and right of the travelers.

A guide pointed to one of the highest mountains. "That steep pyramid is Eiger. The north side is an impossible climb," he said.

When the tourists returned to the train, the windows were closed since the air had grown very cool. Presently they reached Eiger Gletscher station and once more got out.

"What's that?" cried Doris in terror as she heard a roar like thunder not far away.

The girls turned to look. Several gigantic blocks of ice had broken away from the overhanging glacier. They watched as the blocks fell far down into a yawning abyss.

"That certainly had me scared for a moment," Doris confessed.

"Oh, look!" Jean called, pointing. Leaping nimbly over the rocks was a graceful chamois.

"I wonder whether birds ever fly this high," said Evelyn. "Oh, they do!" Two ravens came to rest on the roof of the train. They were almost as large as eagles and cawed loudly.

Jean laughed. "Hello, yourself," she called to them cheerily. A moment later the birds flew away, squawking noisily.

The passengers were ushered aboard another train. This one was heated. The Americans learned the reason for this when they reached a tunnel and were told that for five miles they would be traveling through the mountain. The air was bitterly cold!

Once the train stopped and everyone piled out to walk through a narrow corridor and gaze out of the huge windows which had been carved through the rock. Beyond and below was heavy snow, with white, drifting clouds above.

"According to the guidebook, this is the highest tunnel in the world," Aunt Harriet told the girls. "And it was one of the greatest engineering feats ever attempted."

The rest of the ride did not take long and soon the train reached the Jungfraujoch station. "We're now 11,340 feet above sea level," said Aunt Harriet. "And the glacier here is the largest in Europe."

They followed the crowd into the lowest level of the Berghaus, a combination waiting room, ticket office, and hotel entrance. This amazing structure had been built on solid rock right on the side of the mountain. From its long second-floor porch the visitors gazed at the most breath-taking view they had ever seen. There were vast snow fields covering the Great Aletsch glacier. Rimming it were snow-clad mountains.

"Shall we have an early lunch and then start our sight-seeing?" Aunt Harriet asked. When the girls assented, she led the way to a spacious, pine-paneled dining room with a broad expanse of windows.

"A restaurant on top of the world!" said Doris in awe. "The scenery hardly seems real, does it? More like a painting."

Louise was hardly listening. She was staring out a window. "I just saw Hermann Krisler—I'm sure of it," she whispered excitedly.

"That may mean he has moved out of the chalet!" Jean answered. "Oh, I hope so! Then we could get back to work!"

The Americans were shown to a table by a window. They spent more than an hour over their delicious food. Between forkfuls they kept looking out and discovering an ever-changing panorama caused by the blowing snow and drifting clouds.

When they finished eating, Miss Dana and the girls started their tour of the Jungfraujoch. They walked along a plateau of snow, then entered a covered stairway of snow steps to an underground ice palace. This fabulous place was sixty-five feet below the surface, and had been carved out of the greenish-blue glacier. There were benches, a table with a vase of flowers, a piano, all of ice, and even a stove electrically lighted to make it look real.

"How weird this is!" Aunt Harriet remarked and Doris added, "It almost seems as if human figures of ice should be walking around!"

"I understand the humans are a little distance ahead," said Aunt Harriet with a chuckle.

Presently they emerged into a huge room of ice, its domed ceiling supported by columns. Many tourists were skating and the girls wished they had time to join them, but they were eager to start their climb. Reluctantly, they retraced their steps.

Reaching the plateau again, they walked to where polar dogs were waiting to give sled rides. The animals were harnessed one behind the other. The lead dog was dark in color but the other four were pure white.

"Oh, how beautiful they are!" said Evelyn.

"But not so friendly as the St. Bernards," Jean spoke up.

It was arranged that Aunt Harriet would take a sled ride while the girls climbed to the very tip of the Jungfrau. The foursome went to the sports office to rent equipment.

Louise, first to enter the room, exclaimed in amazement. "Henri!"

The guide, grinning, hurried toward the girls. "I was hoping to catch up with you here," he greeted them.

"You're just in time," said Jean. "Will you take us up to the summit?"

"I certainly will," Henri answered.

In a low tone Louise asked him whether Hermann had come with him. "Oh, no," Henri replied. "He is still at the chalet. But the Feers are watching him closely. He's determined to find the heirlooms, but so far he has had no luck." Henri chuckled. "And I haven't been any help."

Louise did not mention that she thought she had seen Hermann a short time before. When the climbers were ready, they hiked across the level snow, then, chained together, began the ascent of the rocky, snow-covered peak. Henri, in the lead, picked the safest, easiest route. Doris, however, found she was less sure-footed than the other girls.

"I—I'm afraid I can't make it!" she cried out.

"Oh, sure you can," Louise encouraged her.

"But it makes me woozy when I look down."

Henri called, "Don't look down, Doris. Just look up and you'll be all right."

But with each step Doris became more uncertain of her footing. Jean, at the end of the line and directly behind Doris, suddenly gasped.

Doris had lost her balance completely, pitched forward, and was starting to slide down the mountain!

Instantly Jean dug the crampons on her shoes deep into the snow and braced herself hard. At the same time she screamed to attract the others' attention. The three instantly dug in too.

Though the move kept Doris from tumbling farther, the weight of her body swung Jean around and both girls had to be held tightly by the rest until they could get their balance.

"I'm just a nuisance to you," said Doris. "Why don't I untie myself and go back to the Berghaus?"

The others tried to persuade her to go on. Finally, taking courage, Doris said she would.

After that the girls had no trouble.

When they reached the summit the group rested while taking in the magnificent sight. Before them was the blue, snow-free ice of parts of the glacier;

Chained together, they ascended the peak.

below the pure-white snow. Then, farther down, there was brown landscape, then green, mixed with flowers and trees, and finally the villages and lakes.

Henri smiled and pulled himself up very straight. "Whenever I stand here," he said in a hushed voice, "I feel the way I believe my ancestors must have. It is said they always climbed mountains and stood at the summit to give themselves proper humility before God. The vastness and beauty of our Creator's work are shown to fine advantage here!"

The girls nodded. Conversation did not seem appropriate at this moment. Presently Henri turned to leave and they followed him silently down from the summit of the Jungfrau.

When they reached the Berghaus once more, Jean asked Henri, "Is it too late to go skiing for a while?"

"Oh, no," he replied. "We could ski until sunset."

"Then let's do it," Jean urged.

Doris said that she had had enough exercise for one day. Evelyn offered to stay with her and Aunt Harriet while the Danas made a short run.

Henri returned the climbing equipment, and all of them changed their shoes. Then they rented skis and poles and a simple rope-and-pulley arrangement to use for a tow. The trio walked out to the snow-covered glacier and adjusted their skis.

As they reached the starting point, Henri turned

to the girls with a smile. "I don't want to embarrass you," he said, "but I must know how well
you manage on skis."

When the Danas told him they had been skiers
for several years, Henri looked relieved and said,
"As you Americans say, let's go!"

He started off, with Jean following him. As
Louise waited for them to get a little distance
ahead, she saw a man suddenly rise from behind a
huge mass of snow below.

"That's Hermann!" Louise exclaimed to herself.

Then she gasped. Henri was approaching the
snow mass, and it looked to Louise as though
Hermann intended to start an avalanche to bury
his cousin!

CHAPTER XV

Scoundrel on Skis

"Look out!" Louise screamed as loudly as she could. But the wind carried the sound away and it did not reach Henri's ears. Instead, her cry apparently was heard by the man at the top of the great mass of snow. Quickly he ducked out of sight. But Louise was still fearful he intended to harm Henri.

"I must try to stop him!" she thought fearfully. Louise leaned far forward, dug her poles into the snow to give her start a good impetus, then she sped down the slope. To her relief she could see that Henri and Jean had already rounded the promontory of snow and were safe. On impulse, Louise stemmed far to the left to avoid getting into Hermann's trap herself. Nevertheless, she watched carefully for signs of the suspicious man. He was not in sight and Louise breathed a sigh of relief as she took a zigzag course down the glacier in the tracks made by Henri and her sister.

But one eventuality she had not figured on—someone slipping up behind her. Suddenly she became aware of a figure on skis beside her. He grabbed one of her ski poles and ordered her to stop. To avoid a fall, she did just that, then looked up into the eyes of the man who had issued the order.

Hermann Krisler!

"Surprised to see me here, are you not?" he asked, looking down at her through half-squinted haughty eyes.

Louise did not answer. She tried to pull away from Hermann, but his grip was too strong.

"What do you want?" she asked him.

"I have a good idea that you and your sister know where the Krisler heirlooms are hidden. You are going to tell me where right now!"

"If we haven't told Henri, why should we tell you?" Louise countered.

"I think you have told Henri, but he will not tell me."

"If Henri knows," said Louise, "then why hasn't he displayed them or sold them?"

"Your smartness won't do you any good," said Hermann. He started to pull Louise up the slope. "You see that great drift up there where I was standing? It's going to cover you if you don't tell me what I want to know!"

With Hermann's strength, Louise knew that it would not be hard for him to carry out his threat.

Her only hope was that Henri and Jean, missing her, would come back to find her. If she could only stall for time!

Suddenly an idea came to her. She said, "Hermann, it wouldn't be fair for me to reveal the secret to you alone. Henri must hear it. Besides, my sister should be there too. Suppose we ski to the bottom of the slope and talk it over."

Hermann let go of Louise momentarily, as if he were about to agree to her plan. Instantly she took advantage of the opportunity, swerved away from him, and went whizzing down the hill.

Never before had Louise displayed such skill in skiing. She schussed, jumped, and bending low, swept around the turns, following the tracks of those ahead of her.

"My scheme may work," Louise thought hopefully.

From the foot of the slope, where Henri had decided they should end their downhill run, he and Jean looked up in admiration at Louise's performance. Finally she caught up to them. Breathing hard, she stopped within a few feet of where they were standing.

"A magnificent run!" Henri exclaimed. Louise brushed aside the compliment. "That's Hermann Krisler behind me!" she panted. "He threatened me, and he's going to harm you, Henri. Be careful!"

She turned around. To her surprise, no one was

in sight. Had Hermann become frightened and gone back up the slope? Quickly she told her story to Jean and Henri.

"How horrible!" Jean exclaimed indignantly.

Henri's face grew stern. "The actions of my cousin are unbelievable. He is irresponsible. Louise, I am very ashamed that a member of my family should act in such a manner."

"You shouldn't blame yourself," Louise said quickly.

Henri tried to smile, but it quickly faded. "My cousin must have left the chalet right after I did," he remarked. "And I am sorry to say this, but I agree with Louise that Hermann intended to bury me in the snow, and perhaps you girls too—not to kill us but to scare us into telling what he wants to find out."

Jean, who had taken no part in the conversation, now said, "Hermann acts pretty desperate. Does he need money? Is that the reason he is claiming the heirlooms and is so eager to find them?"

"That might be true," Henri replied. "Actually I know little about my cousin's affairs. And now, I believe we should go back and try to find him."

He offered to go ahead up the slope and spike the short tow into the snow for the girls to use.

"Suppose we take turns," Louise suggested.

Following this plan, the guide herringboned to a spot above and the girls pulled themselves up by means of the tow rope to where he was standing.

Then Louise climbed up another hundred and fifty feet and the others pulled themselves up to her.

"My turn," said Jean.

Carrying the tow, she started off. Just as she reached the spot where she was going to push in the heavy spike, she happened to glance up the slope. Some distance ahead lay a man!

As soon as the tow was in place, Jean hurried over to the still figure. "Hermann!" she exclaimed.

"I've broken my leg," the man announced.

"Lie still," said Jean. "As soon as Henri and Louise reach us, we'll put on a splint and carry you to the Berghaus."

Hermann did not thank her for offering to help him. Instead, he began to groan and murmur in German.

When the others reached his side, the three fashioned a makeshift splint of Hermann's ski poles. Then, using the skis and their own jackets, they made a stretcher. Gently they lifted him up and began their side-step climb. The rest of the way to the mountaintop hotel had to be made without the use of the ski tow. The going was difficult, but finally they reached the plateau, then carried him into the hotel lobby.

"I am very grateful to you, girls," said Henri. "I will find a doctor, then take my cousin to a hospital. Please come to the Altberg Chalet to-morrow," he urged.

The girls promised to meet him there, then hurried off to find Aunt Harriet, Doris, and Evelyn. The three were thunderstruck to hear what had happened on the ski run.

"It seems like punishment for that awful man," Doris remarked. "Oh, it gives me the shivers to think you girls might have been buried alive under a snowslide!"

Aunt Harriet felt that her nieces must be exhausted and suggested that they all eat supper at the Berghaus before starting the trip back to Grindelwald.

"That's a good idea," Louise agreed. "I'll go ask Henri if he would like to eat with us while he's waiting for the train to take Hermann to the hospital."

She found him in the lobby. Seeing her, he hurried over and said, "I am very worried about my cousin. He is sicker than we realized. Something must have happened to him on the ski run to make him fall and break his leg. I wish it did not take so long to get to the hospital."

Suddenly an idea came to Louise. "If you want to get him to the hospital quickly, why not ask Edouard Kunkel to fly him there?"

"I will do that!" Henri said enthusiastically.

Louise offered to get in touch with the Kunkel home. Fortunately, she found the pilot there. Edouard said he would take off at once to bring the victim down.

Half an hour later, Edouard landed on the plateau outside the Berghaus. Gently Hermann Krisler was lifted into the plane on a stretcher and Henri climbed up beside him. The Danas waited until Edouard took off, then went to eat their supper.

"This has been a day of surprises and adventures," Aunt Harriet remarked as they started the soup course. Then, smiling, she added, "And I'm glad it is almost over." She looked affectionately at the girls. "I guess I worry too much. You all seem pretty capable of taking care of yourselves."

Doris cast her eyes down. "Everybody except me," she said.

"Don't worry about a little thing like a mountainside spill," Jean told her, chuckling. "It could happen to anyone."

Louise changed the subject. "Tomorrow," she said tensely, "we go back to the chalet and start our search again for those missing heirlooms. I wonder what we'll find inside that hollow beam!"

CHAPTER XVI

A Puzzling Clue

BY NINE o'clock the following morning the Dana girls, together with Doris and Evelyn, arrived at the Altberg Chalet. Henri came outside to meet them, closing the front door behind him.

"The Coxes are here," he said. "We shall have to wait a while before beginning our search. I mentioned that you girls were coming to visit, hoping to hurry their leaving. I even offered to deliver their purchases, but they insisted upon waiting for Herr Feer to pack the souvenirs."

"Oh, phooey!" Doris murmured, and all the girls showed signs of annoyance.

"Henri, how is your cousin Hermann?" Louise asked.

"He is not very well. The doctors decided that he must have had a dizzy spell on the slope. That was why he fell and broke his leg. Apparently the attack was brought on by overexertion. His heart has been affected."

Louise was not surprised to hear this. The fit of temper which Hermann had displayed when he had stopped her on the ski run was enough to upset anybody's physical condition, she decided.

"Hermann confessed," said Henri, "that he heard from a friend in Frankfurt that the Dana detectives were coming here at Rudolph's request. He followed you from Lucerne. Hermann stayed at the chalet to watch your search—a search you didn't make while he was there!"

Louise smiled. Now her reflections turned to the Coxes. It seemed strange that Fred had not come outside to greet the girls in his usual overaffable manner.

Doris had noted this, too, and whispered to Louise, "Fred must be ill!"

The girls were even more amazed at his attitude when they went into the chalet. Mr. and Mrs. Cox and Fred were talking to Herr Feer at the small display cabinet near the door to the kitchen. They did not turn around.

This struck Jean as odd and she winked at the others. Apparently Fred had finally learned that they did not wish to be friends with him!

Herr Feer was packing carved wooden bottle stoppers in a box. They were heads of old and young men, women, bears, foxes, and several held two figures.

Herr Feer tested each one before placing it in the box. By moving a tiny lever on one side of the stopper, the figures were made to go through various motions. A boy and girl on one faced each other and kissed. Two others turned their backs as if angry.

"They're very amusing," Evelyn remarked.

For the first time Fred Cox turned around. He merely nodded at the girls, then went over to another corner of the room and sat down by himself.

"He's really angry at us," Doris whispered.

Instead of talking, Fred gave his full attention to a squirrel bottle stopper which he was holding. The amusing little wooden figurine was sitting up, holding a nut between its front paws. Moving a lever caused it to swish its bushy tail from side to side.

When Doris saw this, she giggled. Fred Cox looked up at her but did not smile in return.

"He's acting like a spoiled child," Doris murmured. "Well, at least he won't bother me any more."

Suddenly the tail of the squirrel dropped off. Fred threw the rest of the bottle stopper to the floor with a vicious snap of his arm, got up from the chair, and strode out of the chalet.

The girls, looking from a window, saw him stalking down the hill. Apparently he was headed for the hotel. They smiled at one another but made no comment.

"Good morning, Frau Feer," Doris called across

the room, as the Swiss woman came in from the kitchen. The other girls greeted her also, then Doris said, "Frau Feer, would you give me a few of your special recipes to take home to Mother?"

"I should be very happy to, Doris. Come into the kitchen."

All this time Henri had been carrying on a one-sided, inconsequential conversation. Now and then the girls would answer. It was very evident that he was trying to fill in the time until the Coxes departed.

But when the box was filled with wooden bottle stoppers and napkin rings ten minutes later, Mrs. Cox said to Herr Feer, "I really must have the rest of the souvenirs I ordered from you. How long will it take you to finish them?"

"They are almost ready. Could you come back for them tomorrow?"

"See here," said Mr. Cox, annoyed, "you've had plenty of time to finish them. I want the whole bunch in half an hour."

Herr Feer stared at his rude customer. The girls were not sure whether he was angry or embarrassed. Finally he said, "I will have them ready in half an hour."

"We will wait," Mr. Cox said. "Hanna, why don't you sit down?"

His wife obediently seated herself in a rocker, picked up a book on flowers, and began to turn the pages.

Mr. Cox stalked out the door. The girls followed, not to join him, but only to take a stroll while waiting for the Coxes to leave. Presently Frau Feer came outside and asked if they would like to pick a bouquet. The girls nodded and separated, looking for choice blooms.

At the back of the chalet, Jean saw Mr. Cox half reclining on the ground, apparently drinking in the view ahead of him.

"They're certainly a queer family," Jean said to herself. Soon she had an armful of flowers and took them to the kitchen.

When the half hour was up, Herr Feer returned to the living room with the balance of the carved wooden figures and packed them neatly in a box. Mr. Cox, who had come back inside, paid the bill. He and his wife said a quick thank-you and good-by to everyone, then walked out to their car.

Jean heaved a sigh of relief. "I thought they'd never go. Now let's get to work!"

She hurried off to get the stepladder. When Henri saw her carrying it into the living room he quickly took the ladder. Setting it in position under the removable beam, he climbed up. After tugging and pulling at the beam for several minutes Henri finally loosened it. The others helped him lower it to the floor.

Quickly they began to examine the beam. It proved to have a panel on the side which had been against the ceiling. There was no sign of an opening in it nor any clue as to how the panel might be removed.

"I guess we'll need a chisel to help us open this," Louise commented.

Herr Feer hurried off to his workshop and brought back a tool kit. With skilled hands he worked carefully so that neither the beam nor anything it might contain would be marred.

"This panel is coming loose!" he said hopefully.

Holding their breaths, the girls waited expectantly. Would there be something of importance inside the hollow beam?

"May I help you?" Henri asked anxiously.

Herr Feer smiled. "I believe that will not be necessary."

One more prying motion of the chisel, and the whole panel came loose. As it dropped to the floor, the eager watchers looked inside the beam.

"There's a paper!" Jean cried out.

Henri leaned down and with excited fingers pulled it out. The yellowed paper was folded over like a letter.

"Perhaps it contains a message," the young man said hopefully.

The others waited politely but impatiently as Henri opened the folded sheet. A look of excitement came over his face.

"I think this is the original of the map we found in Father's papers!" he cried, and held it for the others to see.

Louise took the paper from him. She and Jean pored over it for several seconds. There was the same circle with the radiating lines extending from it. But this one also had other marks. Then Louise said, "This small square in the center— could it mean this chalet?"

Several lines radiated from the square. One was marked "N," probably *nord* for north. At the end of a line which went in a northeast direction there was a tiny square just one third the size of the center square.

"Perhaps the center square does mean this chalet," Henri conceded. "But what does the rest of it mean?"

Louise and Jean suggested that the tiny square at the end of the northeast line might indicate another chalet. "Just a third the size of this one," Louise added.

Henri thought for several moments, then said, "That's in the region of almost perpetual snow. I go into that area every once in a while. If ever there was a chalet at this point, it must have been carried down the mountainside by an avalanche. It's not there now."

The Dana sisters glanced at each other. The same question was going through their minds: Had the missing heirlooms been hidden in this mysterious chalet? If so, perhaps they were lost forever!

Henri did not speak for a long time. He walked back and forth, gazing thoughtfully out first one window, then another. Finally he came back to the group.

"You may be right," he said. "But if the family heirlooms were there, I'm afraid we'll never find them now." The guide suddenly shook off his disconsolate mood. "But maybe they weren't hidden there. Since we found the family shield in this chalet, I believe we may find the rest here."

The Danas, who had felt pretty discouraged during the past few minutes, took heart. And Evelyn, eager for action, asked, "What place do we search next?"

Jean looked at Henri. "Did you ever try the hearth and chimney?"

"No. The stones are cemented in solid. I have tried to pull them out. But I had no luck."

Louise and Jean stared at the massive fireplace, their eyes roving over every inch of it. Finally Jean said, "Henri, will you find a measuring stick? I'd like to compare the two sides of the fireplace. It looks to me as if it's four to six inches wider on the left side."

"That is true," said Henri. "I will get the measure right away."

He returned with a metric measure in a few minutes and the distance was examined. Jean had been correct! One side of the fireplace was fifteen centimeters wider than the other.

"You think something is hidden in that extra space?" Henri questioned her.

"Yes, I do."

On the left side of the fireplace was a deep recess with a window at the end. Against the paneled wall a pine bench with a high back had been built in. Louise pounded on the back, then on the wall above. There was no sound to indicate there was a hollow space behind it.

"I guess this does not mean anything after all," said Henri.

But Jean was not ready to give up. She suggested that they remove the nails which held the high-backed seat to the wall. Again Herr Feer produced tools and started to work. The nails were quickly removed from the room side of the bench, but the back end by the window refused to budge.

"I will get something else," said Herr Feer, hurrying off.

As the others waited, Evelyn walked into the niche to investigate the trouble. Reaching up, she took hold of the high back of the bench and gave it a great tug. Suddenly it gave way.

Evelyn lost her balance and the heavy bench fell over on top of her!

CHAPTER XVII

The Silver Peacock

EVERYONE in the room sprang forward to help Evelyn, pinned beneath the overturned bench. They yanked the heavy, wooden seat out of the way, and assisted the girl to her feet.

"Are you hurt?" Jean asked.

"No, the bench didn't hurt me," Evelyn replied. "But I skinned my knee when I fell." She made a wry face and looked ruefully at the scratched knee, which was beginning to bleed.

Frau Feer offered to bandage the knee. But Evelyn, who was eager to find out whether or not they were on the trail of further heirlooms, thanked her and said that they could do it later.

Everyone turned their attention to the exposed wall. Suddenly Louise exclaimed, "Here's a little door to something!"

Set into the plaster wall was a wooden door about a foot square. It had no handle, so once more the prying tool was brought into action. As the door swung wide, Henri and the others gasped in delight.

Inside was a collection of old silver articles!

"We've found them, Evelyn!" Doris exclaimed. "How marvelous!"

Henri was too overcome to speak. He reached into the opening and one by one handed out the articles. First came an exquisite silver peacock with a long tail, then four ornate candlesticks. Several swords followed.

"Oh," said Doris in awe at the next find. "These cups and saucers are solid gold! And look at all that beautiful table silver!"

Henri smiled. "I can hardly believe my good fortune," he said. Then he gazed nostalgically at the pieces. "I well remember the grand dinners in our castle. Lights, laughter, music— Of course, Rudolph and I were too young to be present, but we were always allowed to take a peek from the stairway."

Suddenly the young man turned red, evidently feeling his listeners might think him silly to have spoken of his childhood. "Shall we hunt in some more places?" he asked abruptly.

"You couldn't stop us!" Jean laughed.

For the next hour, a very intense hunt went on. Floor boards were removed, window sills pried up—every possible hiding place was examined.

Suddenly Louise became aware of a sound which seemed very much like a sob. It was coming from the kitchen. Quickly the girl hurried out there, to find Frau Feer weeping as she polished the silver heirlooms.

Louise rushed up to the woman and put an arm about her. "What is the matter?" she asked kindly. "Have we done something to hurt you?"

Frau Feer gave a convulsive sob. "Our home! Our beautiful chalet! It is being ruined!"

The Dana girl was shocked. Frau Feer was absolutely right! Giving the woman a tight squeeze, she said, "We've all gone crazy! I'll stop this at once."

Louise hurried back to the living room and suggested that the damaging work cease immediately. Everyone was shamefaced. Not only had nothing more been found, but the place was a shambles.

"We must restore this room quickly!" Louise decided.

In an amazingly short time the Altberg Chalet looked as it had two hours before.

Frau Feer had dried her tears and was smiling again. Proudly she brought in the heirloom pieces. Now that they were clean and shiny, their expert workmanship showed off to advantage. Everyone ohed and ahed at their beauty.

"I can just see them gleaming in the candlelight at a great dinner," Doris said dreamily. "Tell us about the Krisler castle, Henri."

The young guide told her the castle was part of an old fortress and stood on a hill.

"Is it a ruin now?" Evelyn asked.

"Oh, no. It is still beautiful to look at."

"Would you like to go back there?"

Henri shook his head. "It is too vast and not homelike. Besides, Switzerland is now my permanent home."

Presently the conversation turned once more to the heirlooms.

"I can't get the maps out of my mind," said Jean. "I'm sure the one we found and the other that Rudolph showed us in Frankfurt indicate the same directions. Before we leave Switzerland, Louise and I should find out if there is a chalet in the area indicated on the map."

"Perhaps you're right," Henri conceded. "We'll look tomorrow if you can get your aunt's permission to make the climb."

"Wonderful!" Jean exclaimed gaily.

When the girls reached the hotel, they learned that Aunt Harriet had gone for a drive with two women staying at the hotel.

The four chums went upstairs and paused in Doris and Evelyn's room to talk about the hidden chalet. "It's just possible," said Evelyn, "that if the Krisler heirlooms were inside the chalet and it was swept away, they may be scattered over the mountainside under the snow."

"Then we'll never find them," Doris said, groaning.

Louise's eyes lighted up. "Maybe we could borrow a St. Bernard to help us find the things."

"Your gray cells are really working," said Evelyn, laughing.

The others were enthusiastic too, so Louise went off at once to telephone Edouard Kunkel. The pilot was not at home, but his mother said that she would give him the message.

"It would be a good idea to have a trained St. Bernard along," she said. "One never knows when there is going to be a snowslide. Those dogs seem to have a presentiment about it. They bark furiously to warn people."

Mrs. Kunkel begged the girls to be careful, remarking that she thought it was a pretty dangerous mission for them.

"We'll have an excellent guide with us," Louise told her. "Don't worry. With both Henri and a St. Bernard, we'll be all right."

On her way from the telephone, Louise saw the hotel manager and stopped to speak to him. "Any news about the owner of the porcelain cow or Mrs. Cox's stolen jewelry?" she asked.

"No," the man answered. "By the way, the Coxes left here suddenly a little while ago."

Louise was startled to hear this. "Why?" she asked.

The manager shrugged. "I am sure the reason

had nothing to do with the service here, because they would have said so." He chuckled as he added, "The Coxes always let you know when they did not like anything, but this time they merely said that they were leaving within an hour and required transportation to Zurich."

At once Louise recalled Fred's behavior at the chalet. Had something occurred which had caused him and his parents to depart suddenly? A feeling of relief came over Louise, and she was sure that Jean and their friends would be happy to learn that the Coxes were no longer at the hotel. On a sudden hunch, the young sleuth had a great desire to investigate their rooms. Perhaps she could pick up a clue to the thrower of the porcelain cow— a clue overlooked by others.

"Have you rented the rooms the Coxes occupied?" Louise asked the manager.

"No, not yet," he replied. "In fact, the rooms have not yet been cleaned."

After a moment's thought, Louise said, "Would you mind if my sister and I searched the rooms? There's just a long chance that we might find some clue to the porcelain cow thrower, or the jewelry thief."

The manager gave his assent, then scribbled a note for Louise to hand to the chambermaid. She hurried upstairs and told Jean what she had in mind. Together the girls found the chambermaid, who unlocked the doors of the recently vacated rooms. Like true detectives, the girls began a minute examination, starting with the room which Mr. and Mrs. Cox had occupied.

Jean, in her thoroughness, pulled everything out of the wastebasket.

Louise laughed. "What do you expect to find there, Sis? That basket has been emptied a dozen times since the cow-throwing episode."

Jean smiled too. "How right you are! But there *is* something interesting in this wastebasket. Look at these whittlings. Mr. Cox must have been busy with a penknife. What do you suppose he was chipping?"

Louise picked up a few of the tiny shavings, then made a guess. "Maybe he was chipping some of those valuable souvenirs he and his wife were taking home to give all their friends. He probably wasn't quite satisfied with Papa Feer's work."

Finding nothing else, the Danas went into the room which Fred Cox had occupied. But after spending ten minutes searching, they uncovered nothing which might be a clue to the thief or to the person who had tried to injure Louise.

When the girls returned to their own room, Aunt Harriet was there. At once they told her about the proposed trip the next day, and eagerly awaited her answer. As Miss Dana weighed the matter carefully, she said:

"I wish your uncle Ned was here to help me decide."

"Oh, I'm sure he'd approve," Jean remarked hopefully.

Finally Aunt Harriet smiled and said, "I understand that Henri is one of the best guides on the mountain. I'll worry while you're gone, of course, but with him looking after you, I guess it will be all right."

The sisters hugged her, then rushed into Evelyn and Doris's room to tell them the good news. At once the four began to make plans for the search.

"Let's talk about it while we eat," Doris suggested. "I'm famished!"

"Good idea," said Jean.

She and Louise returned to their own room to get ready for a late lunch, when a knock came on their door. Jean answered.

A bellhop stood outside. Smiling, he said, "There is a long-distance call for the Dana girls from Frankfurt. It is on the private telephone of our manager. Would you please come down and answer it?"

CHAPTER XVIII

Deceived Detectives

"Your caller is Prince Rudolph Krisler," the manager told Louise and Jean as they entered his office. He pointed to the phone on his desk. "I will leave you alone and see that no one disturbs you." The man left the room, closing the door behind him.

As Jean waited eagerly to learn why the prince was calling, Louise picked up the phone. "Hello."

"Miss Louise Dana?" When Louise said yes, Rudolph went on, "It is good to talk to you again."

"We're so glad to hear from you," Louise said. "We were so upset when you disappeared. Is everything all right now?"

"Oh, yes, and I have a special message for you. I wanted you to hear it before anyone else. My valuable papers have been returned to me."

"Oh, that's wonderful!" Louise exclaimed. "Please tell me about it."

Prince Rudolph explained that the papers had

been returned by mail, so he had no idea who had
sent them. He assumed that it was the man named
Dorfer.

"But the sender kept the map," he went on.
"Did you ever figure out anything about that?"

Louise now brought the prince up to date on
all that had happened, but did so in guarded tones
in case anyone should be listening.

Prince Rudolph was astounded. He started to
speak, then his voice faded away. The sisters were
fearful the connection had been broken, or even
that the young man was being attacked. But soon
they could hear him plainly again.

"Are you all right?" Louise asked worriedly.

Rudolph chuckled. "Yes, fine. I guess there
was some trouble on the line. To get back to what
we were discussing, do I understand that you are
going to continue the search for the family pos-
sessions by climbing the mountain?"

"Tomorrow morning."

"What time?"

"Early."

"I beg of you to wait for me," the prince requested. "I have a strong feeling that you are
about to uncover something very worth while. I
want to be there. Will you wait?"

Louise said that she would be very happy to, but
only if he could come at once. "We must leave
Switzerland very soon," she told him.

"I will take the first plane to Zurich," Rudolph

promised. "And the train or a taxi from there to Grindelwald."

"Then you should be at the chalet before we arrive there tomorrow," Louise told him. "Shall I telephone Henri and tell him you're coming?"

Rudolph chuckled. "I would rather surprise my brother."

"Then we'll keep your secret," Louise said. "Good-by now. See you in the morning."

The following day the girls had an early breakfast in Aunt Harriet's room.

"What are your plans today, Aunty?" Jean asked. "I just hate leaving you so much."

The woman grinned as she held a cup of coffee halfway to her lips. "They include only warm tours," she answered. "A boat trip on the *Thunersee*—Lake of Thun to you—and a lecture and exhibit on wild flowers of Switzerland. But I shall miss you all. I hope you won't be late getting back and I wish you the best of luck."

"Thank you. I have a feeling we'll need it," said Jean.

When the girls finished eating, Aunt Harriet suggested that Louise call a taxi to take them to the chalet. "You'll have a long enough climb from there on," she said.

When they reached the chalet, the girls were surprised not to find Rudolph there. They said nothing and stalled for time as Henri urged that they get started up the mountainside. Finally he could be put off no longer, and Louise told him the secret she had been keeping.

"Rudolph coming!" Henri cried out, his face breaking into a broad grin. "But when?"

Louise told him the entire telephone conversation with Rudolph the evening before. Then suddenly she said, "I hear a car coming now."

"This must be Rudolph!" Henri exclaimed.

But the new arrival was Edouard Kunkel with a huge St. Bernard dog.

The girls rushed out to meet the pilot. "Oh, I knew you wouldn't fail us!" said Louise.

As Edouard stepped from the car, the beautiful dog followed. At once he began to sniff the girls' shoes.

"Brutus is usually very polite," Edouard said, "but he is memorizing your scents in case he should have to rescue you later."

"He's a darling!" Jean leaned down to pat him. "You say his name is Brutus?"

"That's right. He's a brother to Barry and belongs to a friend of mine. He has almost as many rescues to his credit as Barry."

Edouard told the dog to stay with the girls until he returned for him. Brutus wagged his tail, jumped up on the man's chest, and licked his face. Then he got down and went to stand between Louise and Jean.

"He certainly is obedient," Louise remarked, and hugged the great animal.

Edouard wished the group luck on their climb into the snow fields, then stepped back into his car.

"Thanks a million," Doris said to him. "I was a little jittery about this trip, but now everything's all right."

The girls watched as Edouard turned his car and roared off down the mountain. Then Evelyn said, "I wish Prince Rudolph would get here. I'd like to start for that mysterious chalet."

"I wonder what kept him," Louise murmured. "There are many flights out of Frankfurt."

While waiting for the prince to arrive, the girls amused themselves with the dog. They threw sticks at some distance for him to retrieve. But Brutus did not wag his tail nor act as if he were enjoying the game.

"I guess this is kindergarten stuff to him," said Jean, laughing, and called Brutus to her side. "Listen, old fellow," she said, "go find something important. Pick up a treasure!"

The dog looked at her with his mournful expression. Then, as if understanding what she had said, he wagged his tail furiously and began sniffing the ground excitedly. The girls watched in fascination as he bounded a short distance up the slope.

In a few moments the dog stopped, sniffed the earth, and began to dig furiously with his great, front paws. "I believe he has located something," said Jean.

Brutus unearthed a clue to the thief!

All the girls ran to the spot. By this time Brutus was reaching his nose into the little excavation he had made. A moment later he grabbed something in his teeth and stood up.

"Oh, dear," said Doris, "I thought it was going to be one of the Krisler heirlooms."

"What is it?" Evelyn asked.

Brutus laid his find on the grass. Doris was about to exclaim that it was nothing more than a ball of twine, when she changed her mind and shrieked, "*The* twine! The red-and-green ball of twine!"

The girls stared at it. Before their eyes lay the telltale evidence against the jewelry-store thief!

"That makes Mr. Cox guilty!" Jean cried out. "This is the exact same spot where he was sitting yesterday!"

"Mr. Cox *was* the thief!" Louise exclaimed. "He *was* the man I saw go into that Interlaken hotel jewelry store!"

The girls discussed their amazing discovery for several seconds, as the St. Bernard looked on. Finally Jean remembered him and gave the dog a great hug. "You don't know it, Brutus darling, but you've solved a big mystery!"

Doris and Evelyn babbled on about the three tourists who had so completely fooled not only them but the Danas as well. "They weren't dumb and silly at all!" said Doris. "They were just acting. I'll bet Mrs. Cox and Fred are thieves too!"

Evelyn nodded. "Oh, why couldn't we have found them out before this? By now they could be halfway around the world."

The Danas admitted that the bill of sale from the jewelry shop in Lucerne had allayed any suspicion they might have had about Mr. Cox being in Interlaken. "He showed it to us on purpose!" Louise declared. "His wife and son were in Lucerne, while he was busy in Interlaken. And somewhere he changed from a dark to a light suit."

"Very slick," said Doris.

"There's one thing I can't understand," Louise spoke up. "Why did Mr. Cox bother to bury the ball of twine near the chalet?"

"I think I can explain what happened," said Doris. "I didn't tell you before because I didn't think it was important."

Doris explained that while Mr. Cox was standing at the cabinet where the bottle stoppers were displayed, she was in the kitchen. "I told Frau Feer about the clue of the ball of twine. Mr. Cox must have had it in his pocket, and when he heard me, he decided to get rid of the evidence in a hurry. So he buried it on the mountainside, never thinking it would be found."

"We must notify the police at once!" said Louise.

The girls hurried inside the house to tell Henri and the Feers about the discovery. Louise and Jean felt that they should go down to the village and talk personally with the chief of the police, rather than telephone.

"Take my car," Henri offered.

At police headquarters they were ushered into a private room, and quickly told their story to the chief.

"It is amazing!" he said. "I will get in touch with Interpol at once. They will notify all countries to be on the lookout for the Coxes. The three should be arrested soon."

Up to this point Louise had done most of the talking. Now Jean spoke up. "When I was looking through a wastebasket in Mr. Cox's bedroom, I found some tiny wood shavings. Do you think it could be possible that the watches which the Coxes stole were secreted inside the carved wooden bottle stoppers and napkin rings? And then smuggled into the United States?"

The police chief looked at Jean admiringly. "That is a very clever deduction, *Fraulein*. You have probably guessed the truth. I will give out this information also and will let you know the outcome."

Jean told him of the girls' proposed trip up the mountain and said that she would telephone him upon their return to find out if there was any news.

When they returned to the Altberg Chalet, the Danas were concerned to learn that Prince Rudolph had not yet arrived. "What could have happened?" Louise asked worriedly.

Henri said he was afraid another misfortune had overtaken his brother. "Franz Dorfer may have waylaid him again!"

CHAPTER XIX

The Avalanche

As HOUR after hour went by and Prince Rudolph did not arrive at the Altberg Chalet, the Danas and their friends grew more and more worried. Frau Feer served lunch, but no one had any appetite for food.

Henri constantly walked the floor. "I believe I should get in touch with the Frankfurt *polizeiamt*," he said finally. But he was unable to make the connection and resumed his pacing.

During the afternoon, the girls passed the time by doing some searching on the exterior of the building. They had a faint hope that they might discover more clues to the heirlooms, but nothing came to light.

Brutus, who had been frisking about during the search, suddenly began to bark. "I believe someone must be coming!" Jean called out.

The girl listened intently and presently heard

the motor of a car. In another minute a taxi pulled up to the chalet.

"Prince Rudolph!" the Danas cried in unison, as the handsome young man stepped out.

Smiling, he waved at the girls, paid the driver, then came over to shake hands with the group.

"We were so worried about you," said Louise. "We thought Franz Dorfer might have waylaid you again and made you a prisoner."

Rudolph Krisler's eyes twinkled. "Half your guess is right. Dorfer did waylay me, but this time I was the victor."

Jean begged for more details. Rudolph said the smuggler had come to the house where he was staying, and demanded not only money, but an explanation of the crude map.

"This time I was prepared for him." Rudolph chuckled at the recollection and added, "Dorfer is now in jail!"

"I'm certainly happy to hear that," said Louise.

"Please tell us the rest of the story," Jean begged.

Louise interrupted to say that she thought they all should go in the house, so that everyone might hear the whole story. There was an affectionate greeting between the brothers and an exchange of handshakes between the Feers and Rudolph. Then the group sat down and the prince began his story.

He related in detail what had happened from the time he met the girls in Frankfurt.

"Dorfer confessed to everything," Rudolph concluded. "He had mailed back my papers, after he learned they were of no use to him, but he had kept the map. He and Hudson had heard about the heirlooms from a former servant of our family, and were determined to get them. The Interpol had already identified them as thieves and smugglers."

Rudolph turned toward the sisters. "Dorfer remarked that he was getting along all right until you Dana girls spoiled his plans. He was hoping to solve the Krisler mystery himself. When he found that you were coming here, he asked some people who were staying in Grindelwald to keep track of you. They were to keep you from working on the case, if possible, and let him know when you left. Then he was going to move in and hunt for the heirlooms."

"One guess as to who those people were," said Jean. "Was their name Cox?"

Prince Rudolph looked astounded. "You found out they were shadowing you?"

"Well, not exactly that," Jean replied. "In fact, the Coxes fooled us completely on that score. We thought they were three rattlebrained tourists."

Doris told Rudolph of the young man's unwanted attentions to her. "And to think he was trying to date me!" she added in disgust. "All he wanted to do was find out our plans!"

The Danas related the episode of the porcelain

cow and the story of Mrs. Cox's stolen jewelry. "I'm sure now that Mr. Cox hurried back into the hotel and threw that cow at me to keep us from our sleuthing. His wife invented the story of her jewelry as a cover-up."

Henri told his brother about the many carved wooden bottle stoppers and napkin rings which the Coxes had purchased from Herr Feer. "Jean thinks they were secreting stolen watches in them, intending to smuggle them into the United States. But they will never do it now, thanks to the Danas! They'll be caught!"

Louise and Jean blushed a little at the praise, then Louise asked Rudolph if he had any more to tell. "Yes, there's one more part to the story. For Henri and me it is a very important part. I finally located my father's will and everything belongs to Henri and me. Nothing goes to Hermann. Incidentally, I'm afraid both Henri and I suspected our cousin Hermann of being mixed up with Dorfer and Hudson. But Dorfer exonerated Hermann completely, so he is at least clear on that score."

"Thank goodness," Henri murmured softly. The others too were glad to hear that Hermann was not involved in the smuggling racket.

Prince Rudolph was told about his cousin's illness and said he would go to see him soon. "All Hermann needs is a job. He is too much of an idler, and that gets him into trouble."

The conversation now turned to the climb up the mountain to the mysterious chalet indicated on the map. Henri said he had little hope that it was still there, but that possibly they would find the foundation. He smiled boyishly. "And even some of the heirlooms if they had been buried in the cellar."

Though eager to begin the search, Louise said, "I guess it's too late to start our climb today, isn't it?"

"I'm afraid so," Henri answered. "But let's plan to go early tomorrow morning."

When the girls arrived at the Altberg Chalet just after eight o'clock the following day, Frau Feer presented the climbers with sandwiches and thermos bottles of hot chocolate. With the Feers waving and wishing the group luck and the St. Bernard bounding ahead, the mountaineers started off. They took the northeast trail as indicated on the map.

To save their strength and breath, the climbers held little conversation, confining it to rest periods. Up they went, leaving the green fields behind, then hiking across the brownish area. When they reached the snow line, they put on their heavy sweaters and jackets.

Their progress was slowed down considerably, but Brutus was happy and excited. Every so often he would give a low growl, then start digging furiously. In a few moments he would bring up

some object. Each time the climbers would wait
expectantly to see what it was, then sigh in disappointment. The St. Bernard's treasures included
lost gloves, caps, and finally a canteen.

"Oh, Brutus, please find something important!"
Jean pleaded.

The dog wagged his tail, gave a short bark, and
bounded off as if to obey Jean's request. But another hour of climbing went by without the St.
Bernard locating any object or the climbers getting any glimpse of a chalet.

Then Henri, who was in the lead, shouted back
to the others, "I see the roof of a building!"

Everyone tried to put on speed but it was all
they could do to lift their boots in and out of the
heavy drifts. They crossed a small, rounded peak
and started down the other side.

"I see it!" Evelyn exclaimed to the other girls,
pointing.

*Nestled in the snow below them was a tiny
chalet!* The lower section was still buried, but the
upper part, with an unusually long gable and
heavily carved decoration, stood out clearly in the
sunlight.

"The map was right!" Prince Rudolph cried out
excitedly.

As the climbers gathered in front of the building with the St. Bernard, they gazed at it in amazement. How had it managed to withstand an avalanche?

"Do you suppose Anna and Fritz built it?" Rudolph asked Henri.

His brother confessed to being completely puzzled. Furthermore, only a month before he had climbed in this very area.

"The chalet was not showing at that time," he declared. "Recent strong winds must have blown the snow away from around part of the building."

The group, eager to enter the half-hidden chalet, beat a path to the door. There was no lock; instead, a long wooden bar kept the door from being blown open.

Rudolph and Henri, using great strength, finally lifted the bar from the slot. Then, pulling with all their might, they opened the door.

The brothers stood back so that the girls might enter first. To their astonishment, the one-room, windowless interior was amazingly dry and free from sifting snow. The hut was crudely furnished.

"How can we prove this might be the chalet where some of your heirlooms are hidden?" Louise asked the Krislers.

Before answering, Rudolph and Henri walked around and looked at various utensils. Suddenly the guide stopped and pointed. "Here is proof." Chiseled into the bottom of a wooden bowl were Anna's initials.

"Let's start our hunt," Evelyn urged. She opened a drawer in the crude table, but found only knives and forks in it.

Doris unfastened a chest in one corner of the room. In it were woolen scarfs, caps, and mittens. She rummaged through them.

"No heirlooms here," Doris announced.

Louise and Jean were examining a crude stove, filled with wood ashes.

"Maybe some of the heirlooms are buried in the ashes," said Jean. The ashes were removed a cupful at a time, but no object was found.

Rudolph and Henri, meanwhile, had been busy examining the heavy, wood-paneled walls. They pounded and knocked. Finding nothing to indicate that any heirlooms were hidden behind them, they next tried the floor boards.

"Here is one that looks different from the others," Prince Rudolph remarked.

As they pried it up, he suddenly exclaimed, "Henri, this is a jewel case!"

Eagerly he lifted it out and together the brothers swung up the lid. Inside lay a dazzling array of exquisite rings, necklaces, and bracelets!

"They're magnificent!" Jean exclaimed.

"Our mother's jewelry!" Henri cried out. "This is the most valuable and important part of the Krisler heirlooms."

As Louise and Jean bent forward to admire the beautiful pieces, Brutus began to bark excitedly outside the chalet. The sisters ran outside. Perhaps callers were coming! Would they prove to be friendly or not?

"I don't see or hear anyone," remarked Jean, looking down along the trail which they had broken.

"No, but don't forget that Brutus can detect a person from far away," her sister said.

The St. Bernard continued to bark and was already bounding away.

"He certainly is excited about something," Jean insisted.

Suddenly Louise frowned. "Jean, maybe Brutus is trying to warn us of a snowslide that's about to start. We'd better get back into that cabin quick!"

The sisters ran toward the cabin as fast as they could. But they did not reach it in time. A huge mass of snow came roaring down the mountainside. In a second the girls were completely covered!

CHAPTER XX

A Treasure Revealed

DURING the moments when the snow was piling on top of the Danas they struggled frantically to keep it from packing tightly around them. But their efforts were futile.

"We'll be suffocated!" they told themselves in panic.

Wild thoughts ran through their minds. Why did everything have to end this way? What a tragic way to leave Uncle Ned and Aunt Harriet who had given so much of their time and love to rear them!

Suddenly Louise became aware that the snow around her face was being furiously dug away. In a moment she was able to open her eyes. The great, kindly face of Brutus was revealed for a second, then it disappeared.

"You blessed dog!" Louise murmured.

The great St. Bernard had leaped toward Jean and was now pawing frantically to uncover the girl's head. In a few moments he accomplished this, then dug from around Jean's shoulders until her arms were free.

"You've saved my life, old fellow!" she whispered.

Drinking in great gulps of air, Jean was able, with the dog's help, to move about. Then both began working on the imprisoned Louise. Soon she too was standing up. Both girls hugged the great St. Bernard.

"You're marvelous!" Jean sobbed.

"The most wonderful dog in all the world," Louise added. Brutus stood by quietly as Louise said, "I hope Doris, Evelyn, and the Krisler brothers are safe."

As she spoke, both girls turned toward the chalet. It was almost completely buried.

"We must help them get out," said Louise. "We left the door open. No telling how much snow got inside. Oh, how I wish I had a shovel!"

At this moment the sisters became aware of the sound of a plane.

"It looks like Edouard's!" Jean exclaimed.

"Yes," said Louise. "I'll bet Aunt Harriet sent him to check on us! Am I glad to see him!"

The plane circled the area several times, then swooped down toward them. It landed gracefully on a plateau which stretched beyond the chalet and the pilot braked to a stop in the deep snow on the plane's skis.

Edouard Kunkel stepped out. He hurried forward and surveyed the recent avalanche in horror. "Thank goodness you are safe."

"But we're worried about the others," Louise told him. "They're inside the cabin. Have you a shovel in your plane?"

"Indeed I do," Edouard replied. "I'll get it."

The young pilot set to work with a will. The snow flew furiously from side to side as he drove a deep wedge through the drift. Brutus worked frantically with his great front paws and helped to clear the path.

In ten minutes they reached the doorway and plowed through the great drift which had settled in the room. Wedged in the corner were Rudolph, Henri, and the two girls.

"You're all right!" the four cried together upon seeing Louise and Jean, and Doris added, "We were frantic about you."

As Edouard continued to shovel, with Brutus and the Danas doing all they could to assist, the four prisoners were finally released.

"We had better go out to the plateau and talk about getting away from this place," said Edouard, after he had been introduced to Rudolph.

He led the way, with Doris and Evelyn behind him. But Rudolph, Henri, and the Danas did not follow at once. The men searched in the snow until they found the case of jewels which had been knocked from their hands.

Suddenly Louise noticed that part of a wall panel had bulged out, evidently from the weight of snow and ice. She reached up and gave the panel a yank.

Everyone gasped. Behind the panel stood a huge encrusted silver wassail bowl, with many cups and a ladle.

"The last of the missing heirlooms!" Prince Rudolph cried unbelievingly.

"And to think we almost missed this!" Jean burst out.

Rudolph and Henri made their way to Louise's side. Henri lifted out the cups and ladle, while his brother took the bowl. There were exclamations of admiration from the onlookers. Then everyone started for the door.

"I can hardly believe our good fortune," Henri said. "When we get back to the Altberg, we must have a great celebration!"

Assured now that all the heirlooms had been recovered, the Danas and the Krisler brothers worked their way out through the narrow passage in the snow until they came to Edouard's plane. The waiting group was astounded at the latest find.

After discussing the Krislers' great luck a few moments, Edouard said, "I was just telling Doris and Evelyn that I think I had better fly all of you out of here. Suppose I take Evelyn and Doris first. They are pretty cold."

The others agreed. As the two girls stepped into the plane, Edouard said, "We'll all meet at the chalet."

The plane took off and the others began to discuss the whole amazing mystery. They were still talking about it when Edouard returned. This time Louise and Jean became his passengers. They took Brutus with them and in a short while they were at the Altberg Chalet, warming themselves and drinking some of Frau Feer's delicious broth. Brutus was busy eating five pounds of beef.

"You certainly earned that, old fellow," Jean told him. "Louise and I owe our lives to you."

When Rudolph and Henri returned, Edouard said that he must leave to return the St. Bernard to his friend. Reluctantly, the girls said good-by to the beautiful dog. In the many mysteries they had solved, they had never met such an endearing and brave animal.

"We'll never forget you," Jean said to Brutus, as they walked outside with him. "And every time we play with the St. Bernard puppy we're going to get, we'll think of you!"

The dog wagged his tail, then he sat down and put up his right paw as if to shake hands. The girls took it and hugged him. Then Brutus jumped into the plane. In silence, the girls watched until the craft was out of sight.

As they turned back to the chalet, a taxi pulled up and Aunt Harriet Dana stepped out. "Oh, you're back! I'm so relieved—I've worried every minute since you left this morning."

The girls decided not to tell her yet about their harrowing experience. That could come later. For the moment they just wanted her to know that all the Krisler heirlooms had been found.

"I'm so happy to hear that," Aunt Harriet said. "Now I guess every angle of the mystery has been solved."

"Do you mean that the Coxes—?" Louise asked.

Aunt Harriet nodded. "The police caught them in Rome, Italy." She looked at her nieces admiringly. "Everything you surmised about them was true, and the police sent word to thank you for uncovering a smuggling ring that had defied authorities for some time."

"Those horrid Coxes even lent some fun to our adventure," said Jean. "Louise, do you realize the mystery is at an end? What are we going to do now?"

"There'll be school pretty soon," Doris reminded them. But before classes started, Louise and Jean found themselves involved in a fascinating case, **THE HAUNTED LAGOON.**

Now, at the chalet, Frau Feer, with the help of the girls and Aunt Harriet, prepared a luscious feast. As the whole group gathered at the long table, Prince Rudolph, seated at the head, called on each of the guests to make a short speech. Some of the talks were solemn, some humorous, but the one which the Danas liked best came from Henri.

"It is going to be most difficult to say good-by to the finest Americans I have ever met," he said, smiling at them. "Rudolph and I are making a request of you. May we come to see you in your own country?"

As all the girls said, "Oh, please do!" Doris murmured, "To think that we'll have not only one, but two princes to introduce to our friends at Starhurst School!"